Caves, Cannons and Crinolines

By Beverly Stowe McClure

Twilight Times Books
Kingsport Tennessee

Caves, Cannons and Crinolines
This is a work of fiction. All concepts, characters and events portrayed in this book are used fictitiously and any resemblance to real people or events is purely coincidental.

Paladin Timeless Books, an imprint of
Twilight Times Books
Kingsport TN
http://twilighttimesbooks.com/

First Edition: June 2010

Library of Congress Cataloging-in-Publication Data

McClure, Beverly Stowe.
  Caves, cannons, and crinolines / by Beverly Stowe McClure. -- 1st ed.
    p. cm.
  Summary: In 1863 Vicksburg, Mississippi, outspoken fourteen-year-old Lizzie Stamford yields to her secret desire to join the Confederate Army disguised as a boy, but she quickly learns that neither war nor all Yankees are what she believed them to be.
  ISBN-13: 978-1-60619-112-5 (trade pbk. : alk. paper)
  ISBN-10: 1-60619-112-8 (trade pbk. : alk. paper)
  1. Mississippi--History--Civil War, 1861-1865--Juvenile fiction. [1. Mississippi--History--Civil War, 1861-1865--Fiction. 2. Sex role--Fiction. 3. Family life--Mississippi--Fiction. 4. Conduct of life--Fiction. 5. Vicksburg (Miss.)--History--Siege, 1863--Fiction.] I. Title.
  PZ7.M13375Cav 2010
  [Fic]--dc22

                                    2010013805

Cover artwork by Ardy M. Scott

Printed in the United States of America.

For Mom and Dad and my brother Arwood in heaven.
For my sister Linda, an inspiration.
And for Jack, my soulmate.

Chapter 1

DEAREST BROTHER WILLIE,

We went to the cave for the first time today—
Mama, Nat, and I. And I hate it! I prefer to risk injury
from the hissing, screaming shells in my house than to
scurry underground like a scared rabbit. Papa is at the
hospital, attending the sick and wounded. We see him
so seldom these days. Sometimes I wish he were not
a doctor. Then he could stay home with us, where he
belongs.

I hate what this war has done to our family. You and
Joseph are far away, in Virginia. I miss you all terribly.
Mama worries about you. She worries about Papa. She
scarcely lets me out of her sight. Most of my friends
have left Vicksburg for safer places. The ones remain-
ing are living in caves or basements. I'm supposed to
watch Nat. Mama fears he will run away to find you. I
know he shan't do such a thing. Every time a shell falls,
he hides. The war confuses gentle Nat. He does not
comprehend why men kill each other. Neither do I.

We heard the Yankees have taken Jackson. Our
army fell back to the Big Black River and then retreated to Vicksburg. Their return was a sad sight. Wagons,
cannon, and ambulances clattered down the streets.
Ragged and weary soldiers, some with arms in slings,
some leaning on crutches, others carrying the wounded,
stumbled alongside them. We gave the men what food
and water we could spare, which was very little. Many

blamed General Pemberton for our defeat. Others said
the fault was not his. Jefferson Davis must have confidence in him, or he would not have put John Pemberton in charge of defending Vicksburg, would he? I have
met General Pemberton and think he has courage.

Vicksburg has been under siege now since the eigh-
teenth of May. Gunboats on the Mississippi bombard
us from the west. Parrott shells rain down from the
hills to the east. We are caught in the middle. Nowhere
is safe, not even the caves, like Mama says. You'd think
General Grant would know better. He has tried to con-
quer our city before, without success. No matter. Our
soldiers will send those Yankees scuttling, their tails
tucked between their legs like scared dogs.

Mama and some of the women made bandages for
the wounded last night. Oh! I must tell you what happened this morning. I was asleep in my bed when a
shell burst through the roof and tore a hole in the wall
above me. The house rocked like a baby's cradle, until
I thought it would fall down around my ears. Nat and
Mama rushed in to see if I was injured. Nat, being Nat,
dug the shell out to add to his collection. He has quite
a few. Why he wants them heaven only knows.

When Mama saw my damaged room, she panicked
and skedaddled us to the cave. We've been here ever
since, and it's near evening. I had no time to get my guitar or my books. My piano surely will be ruined. These
Yankees! Have they no manners? Would they wish us
to destroy their homes? I think not.

Nat tugs at my arm. He has something to show me,
so I'll close. Tell Joseph I shall write him later. If I were
a boy, I'd fight the Yankees with you. Does a girl love
her home and family any less than her brothers do?
Does she not have pride, honor? It angers me that girls
are not allowed to defend what is theirs.

Mama would faint away if she heard me talking this way. I'm supposed to be a lady she reminds me every day.

"Why?" I ask her.

"Because you are," she says. A truly puzzling answer.

My love and prayers go with you.

Always,
Lizzie

I turned to Nat, crouched beside me without the mouth of the cave, his chin on his knees. "What is it, Nat?"

He placed a small piece of wood in my hands. "I made this for you, Lizzie," he said in his slow, easy way.

"My piano," I said, surprised at the perfect details of his miniature carving, though I really shouldn't be. Nat is good with his hands. He can turn even a boring scrap of wood into a thing of beauty. "It's exquisite."

He held out another carving, a boat, like the gunboats on the Mississippi, save his had sails. "Someday I'm going to build a whole fleet and sail around the world," he said.

I believed he would. Nat is shy and a dreamer, and others think he is slow and not quite right in the head. In fact, he is the smartest in our family. Even though he's only twelve, two years younger than I am, he's half a head taller. He will be a big man, like our father. I ruffled Nat's hair, the color of the fields when the grain turns golden, the same as Papa's and Joseph's. Willie and I resemble Mama, our eyes the green of the forest, our hair as brown as the soil.

"Captain Nathan Stamford," I said. "Very impressive."

A sudden rushing sound filled the air, and Nat cringed against me, his hands over his ears. "Here comes another one," he said softly.

A woman and her two children darted to a nearby cave. All up and down the bluffs, men, women, and little ones ducked for cover. A shell exploded, sending a flame of fire to earth directly in front of us. The noise threatened to burst my eardrums. The ground trembled as shell fragments scattered.

Nat pressed closer. "Will it ever stop?"

I put an arm around him. "Yes," I said, but I wasn't sure.

Another shell screamed past, and Mama rushed from the cave. "Elizabeth! Nathan! Have I raised children without sense enough to come in out of the storm? Inside! Hurry!"

Nat leapt to his feet and immediately vanished within that hideous animal den, but I did not fancy spending the night in a hole in the ground. I lingered and, forgive my disrespectful tongue, found myself saying, "It's not a storm, Mama. It's the Yankees."

Mama had this way of twisting her mouth just so, the way she did now, a warning that she was losing patience. "Must you argue with everything I say, Elizabeth?"

"I'm not arguing. It's the truth."

She tucked a wisp of my hair behind my ear. "This is difficult for all of us, honey," she said. "Come inside. We must talk."

I gave the deepening blue sky a last look and trailed after her. Halfway inside I halted, my hands clenched at my sides. I could not stay in this coffin to be buried alive. I spun around.

"Elizabeth!"

I turned back. "Yes, Mama?"

"Please, sit down. You too, Nathan."

She eased into the rocking chair Papa had brought, along with a small table and mattresses, soon after he had hired the cave dug in the hillside behind our house. Cave digging had become quite a profitable business in Vicksburg lately. Papa paid fifty dollars for ours. Imagine that much money for a hole in the ground, another senseless part of this war. Since there were no other chairs, Nat and I dropped to the floor at Mama's feet. She flicked open her lace fan, moved it slowly, back and forth, and rocked for a moment, collecting her thoughts.

Finally she said, "I know not whether I shall ever become accustomed to the cannon, the mortars, and the changes the Federals have brought to our lives. I'm inadequate at making decisions. How I wish your father were here to offer his advice, but he isn't. So..."

The rocking chair stopped. Mama straightened my shawl about my shoulders. "This morning frightened me, Elizabeth. If that shell had fallen inches lower …" She shook her head, took a shuddery breath. "I shan't think about that. You were spared this time, honey, but your narrow escape made me realize our home is an easy target for the Federals. So I've decided we'll live here, until our army drives them from Vicksburg."

Live in the cave? What a horrid thought. "But Mama—"

Her mouth twisted for the second time. "I have some mending to do now," she said. "You are to stay inside the cave, Nathan, Elizabeth. Understand?"

"Yes, Mother," Nat said.

I said nothing.

Mama looked at me. "Elizabeth?"

She knew my sometimes-rebellious nature well.

"I understand," I mumbled. But I never said I would.

Apparently satisfied, Mama lit a candle and went behind the blanket hanging from the ceiling, separating her bedroom from the living area, leaving Nat and me alone.

She was asking the impossible. Already, the walls were closing in around me. The cave was darker than a tomb. The only light, since Mama had taken the candle, came from the flash of shells, the moon, and the stars. My mattress was in one corner, but I'd get little rest there. A more miserable place to live in I could not imagine. I glared at Nat, accusing him, which wasn't fair. Very little was, these days. For instance, Nat stayed up half the night, spending hours studying the stars, so Mama had not objected when he laid a blanket to sleep on at the cave's entrance, and I was stuck in a dreary corner.

"I can't do this, Nat," I said. "I can't."

"You can do whatever you have to, Lizzie. Even get along with the spiders."

"Spiders!"

I could not decide whether to laugh or cry. Here I was, suffocating in the dark, and we had bugs, too. I dared not move, but other things wiggled on the floor. I saw them. "Nat!" I screamed and stomped at a monstrous brown bug.

He bent down and plucked up the bug. "Congratulations, Lizzie. You smashed a pebble."

I slapped his shoulder. "You are not amusing." I picked up my skirts. "I will not share my bed with ... wild things. I'll sleep under the stars."

"You heard Mother. We're to stay in the cave."

"You're outside."

"I'm guarding the entrance."

"What against? Bugs?"

Nat frowned. "You are upset, aren't you, Lizzie? Don't be. Most insects and spiders are harmless."

"You say."

"If it makes you feel better, I'll search your mattress." On his hands and knees Nat examined every inch. Then he declared my bed bug free.

I pointed to what appeared to be a large hairy spider. "What is that?"

"Tree roots."

"Those look like eyes to me."

"Listen, Lizzie, leave the spiders and insects alone, and they'll leave you alone."

"Do they know that?"

His frown switched to a sweet smile. "They do. I told them. But on the chance you feel anything crawling on you during the night, holler. I'll come running."

Holler? What good would that do? Resigned to my fate, at least for the present, I lay down and stared at the shadows from the fiery shells, playing across the ceiling of dirt. How I longed for my four-poster bed, with its canopy top, and for my walls, with the blue flowered wallpaper. In spite of Nat's assurance that no spiders occupied my bed, my arms itched with imaginary crawling things. I scratched. And thought. And planned.

For I intended to join the Confederate Army, like my brothers, Willie and Joseph.

12

Chapter 2

IT WASN'T THE SPIDERS that helped me make my decision. It wasn't even the cave. It was something deeper, something inside me that rebelled at the thought of cowering in this burrow, while my brothers fought for our home, for our beliefs. Even though I'm a girl, I am a Stamford. I shall do the same.

The sound of musket fire, a baby's cry, a temporary lull broken by the wind's song echoed in my ears, mingled with my thoughts. I dared not tell Nat my plans. He'd think I was abandoning him and try to talk me out of it. Best to wait until everyone had retired and then slip away. I'd leave Mama a note, so she wouldn't fret. I sighed, knowing she would anyhow.

It seemed hours before Nat settled down. At last, when nobody was stirring, I rose and crept to the entrance. The servants—Aunt Lois, thin as a silk thread, and Uncle Morris, tall and white-headed—slept alongside Nat, their satiny black skin blending with the shadows. They aren't really my aunt and uncle, but my brothers and I have always called them this, out of respect. They're family. They've cared for me since the day I was born. Aunt Lois nurses me when I am ill. Uncle Morris teaches me to work in the garden and grow delicious vegetables. They praise me when I play the guitar or piano or do something good. They reprimand me when I leave my clothes on the bed or floor, instead of putting them away in the armoire, or when I behave unladylike, which is most of the time, according to them.

"Good-bye, Aunt Lois, Uncle Morris," I whispered. "Pray for me."

Quickly, before they awoke, I stepped over Nat, flat on his back, snoring lightly, and into the fresh air. I paused a moment to breathe in the sweet scent of crepe myrtle, passionflower, and magnolia, a welcome reprieve from the musty cave. My mistake.

"Where you going, Lizzie?" Nat asked, behind me.

I had forgotten how lightly he slept. "Um … for a walk," I said, for that was all I could think of.

He moved in front of me. "A young lady does not wander the streets in the middle of the night without a chaperone," he said.

Normally shy around others, Nat spoke his mind with me, unfortunately. I gritted my teeth at his stubbornness, a trait that ran in our family. Grasping his hand I yanked him away from the cave, to keep from disturbing the servants. "A young gentleman does not tell his older sister what she can and cannot do."

"When his sister puts herself in danger he does." Nat inclined his head toward the crack of gunfire coming from the rifle pits. Even though we could not see them, Papa had told us some of the ditches where the fighting took place were less than two miles from town. "Yankees are out there, Lizzie," Nat said.

"The roof of the cave might collapse on me, too, the way the Ridgley's roof did." My voice rose an octave. "The men had to dig them out, remember?"

Nat remained calm. "Girls do not fight in wars."

He suspected what I was about to do, or else he was guessing. Either way, I'd have to wait until another night. Without admitting a thing and speaking as softly as he, with some difficulty, I asked, "Why not?"

"Because … because they're girls."

A truly male observation.

ଔଔ

Disappointed by my failure to escape and wondering if another opportunity would present itself, or if I was trapped in this dreadful cave for the rest of my life, I tossed this way and that on my mattress. I received some satisfaction from the fact that Nat was restless as well. I know, for I heard his footsteps, pacing. In the hills, a voice wailed. In pain? The staccato pop of rifle shots sent a tremor through me. I burrowed my face in my pillow and thought of Joseph and Willie, on a battlefield somewhere in Virginia.

"Stay safe," I prayed. "Come home soon."

Once, I had overheard Papa telling Mama about his patients who died from infected wounds. Sometimes the soldiers were brought to the hospital too late. Other times Papa held a hand for comfort, until the gallant soul took his final breath. Finally, I slept and dreamed of Willie, just seventeen, and Joseph, nineteen. I dreamed of Patrick, their friend and mine, who went with them but became sick with the yellow fever, never to recover.

My mattress shifted as someone sat down, snapping me from my dreams. "Aunt Lois says breakfast is prepared."

I blinked one eye partway open, flicked a hand at Nat. "Go 'way," I said, still annoyed with him for interfering with my plans last night. Besides, I could not swallow another bite of cornbread and bacon. Cut off as we were from the rest of the world, thanks to the Yankees who controlled the river and the fact that the railroad tracks were partly destroyed, our supplies were scarce. As a consequence, our meals consisted of bacon and cornbread three times a day and milk from a neighbor's cow. Occasionally Aunt Lois made biscuits from the small supply of flour we had left, but without soda they were tough and hard to chew. I expected to break a tooth each time I ate one. And vegetables and fruit were almost impossible to procure.

I pulled my blanket over my head. "I'm not hungry."

"I hear your stomach rumbling."

I could not deny the obvious. Yawning, I peeled off the covers and sat up. The cave had not improved since yesterday. I was choking already. Immediately, a new plan began to form in my mind. After breakfast concluded, I would beg Mama for permission to fetch my books and my guitar to the cave. If she did not ask Nat to accompany me, I would soon be in the army. If she did, well, I'd think about that should it happen. I stood and slipped my dress over my chemise, not bothering to put on my hot, bothersome crinoline. I felt ten pounds lighter without it.

Nat looked at the ceiling, his face redder than the sunset.

I laughed, enjoying his embarrassment. He deserved it, the toad. I ate quite a bit, considering I wasn't hungry.

But Mama's reply to my request was a sharp "No!"

Later, she sent Nat and Uncle Morris to the house for our toothbrushes, books, and other personal items, including my guitar.

"My brothers get to do exciting things," I mumbled and grumbled, "and I'm stuck with dishes and sewing. What an awful bore. Oh, I wish I were a boy!"

Aunt Lois clucked her tongue and gave me that look, very much like the one Mama often gave me. I lifted my chin in defiance. "Well, I do."

Aunt Lois smiled. "I knows it, Miss Elizabeth. But you isn't a boy. Makes no sense to wish for it then, does it?"

Such words of wisdom. She always managed to lift my spirits. "Not a bit," I said.

I had dusted the table and was putting Mama's thread in her workbox when hoofbeats echoed on the street in front of our house, and a courier rode up the hillside with a message. Since Mama was in her room, pinning up her hair, I took it. On the way to deliver the note, I peeked inside. I only read the first line before I cried, "Mama!" and skipped into her room, my heart lighter than gossamer.

"Elizabeth! Good heavens! What is wrong?"

I thrust the note at her. "Nothing's wrong. Everything's right. Papa's coming home."

Mama read the message, smiled. Then she slapped her hand to her cheek. "He is! Today! Oh my! Your father expects to find us at the house. He doesn't realize it's damaged. I'll have to send word–"

Refusing to let the opportunity pass to leave this disgusting hole, I interrupted quite rudely. "The cave is much too small for Papa. Why, the ceiling is so low he'll have to bend over, and he'll have a terrible backache from it. He'll be much more comfortable at home, even with its injuries."

Mama skimmed an anxious look around. "I hadn't considered that. You may be right, honey. I'm hesitant, though. The thought of being in the midst of cannon fire, not knowing where the next shell will strike, gives me a headache. Still ..."

She was wavering. I handed Mama her bonnet and parasol. "If we hurry, we can catch Uncle Morris and Nat before they leave the house." I put on my own bonnet.

"Your father is quite large," Mama said. "The poor man works so hard. He needs to be able to rest." She made up her mind. "Yes. We'll return, at once."

In minutes, Aunt Lois, Mama, and I had crossed the cool, shady ravine and covered the short distance to our house. Mama paused at the black wrought-iron gate leading to the front veranda. "Go on ahead, Lois. Elizabeth and I will be in soon."

She straightened my crooked bonnet. "You and Nathan were engaged in quite an argument last night, honey. Your voice was raised."

She had heard us. What exactly had she heard? Hopefully, not everything. "We weren't quarrelling, Mama. We just had a difference of opinion."

She wasn't convinced. "Honey, Nathan confides in you. Unless I'm mistaken he mentioned fighting and war. He's not considering enlisting in the army, is he?"

The idea of Nat in the army was ridiculous; but at least Mama didn't suspect I was the one he meant. She had enough worries with Willie and Joseph and Papa, without adding Nat to her concerns. I had to set her mind at ease. "Nat would never enlist, Mama. The cannon and muskets terrify him. Anyhow, he's too young."

"Boys his age have joined," she said.

"Nat would never."

"Then why were you arguing?"

I meant to be honest with her, I truly did, but sometimes it's better if a person doesn't know the whole truth. For Mama's peace of mind, I fabricated a story, a fairly convincing one, I might add. The words rolled off my tongue, smooth as honey. "I couldn't sleep and went outside for air. Nat came to see if I was all right."

A wrinkle line formed between Mama's eyes. "Are you all right?"

A hard knot gripped my middle. Was it guilt or the greasy bacon I had eaten earlier? My mouth tripped along, saying what it wanted. "I'm fine. Are you?"

"I'm doing the best I can." Mama's voice trembled.

That knot twisted deeper, burrowing into my very soul. The bacon was not to blame for the ache in my stomach. I had never lied to Mama or Papa. I couldn't now. I was ready to confess, no matter the consequences. "Mama—"

She kissed me on the cheek. "Thank you for easing my mind about Nathan, honey. With my family scattered hither and thither, you and your brother are all that keep me sane these days."

I swallowed my confession.

Chapter 3

THE THREE-STORY HOUSE was the prettiest sight I had ever seen. I felt like I had been away for a year, instead of a day. Even though one of the black shutters was splintered into fragments, and Mama's flowers lay in the soil, crumpled heaps of leaves and faded blossoms destroyed by the shells littering the yard, my spirits rose. We could repair the shutters. We could plant more flowers, after the Yankees left. We were home. Papa would be home soon. For now that was enough.

Sometime during the night, a shell had broken through the kitchen wall, skipped across the hall to the dining room, and damaged the table. Nat had it upside down and was patching the leg.

Uncle Morris looked up from picking up pieces of plaster. "Dem Yankees done make one big mess, Miss Elizabeth," he said with a scowl.

"They did," I agreed, and started gathering up the cloth napkins and pieces of plates and glasses that had been on the table, before the shell dashed them to the floor.

Mama knelt to help me. "My lovely china," she said, running a finger over a crack in a saucer. "Will we have nothing left? Are there no gentlemen in the Federal Army? Their mothers would hang their heads in shame to behold their sons' disgraceful behavior. Myself, I fancy taking a willow switch to those scalawags who did this and tan their backsides until they cannot sit."

I believed she would, given the chance. In my mind I pictured a Yankee soldier bent over Mama's knee, the switch leaving red marks on his white skin, revealed for the world to see. Susan Stamford, southern born, proper lady, had accepted the role this war forced upon her, though reluctantly. In some ways I think she is stronger than my brothers or my father. She might even comprehend why I have to defend my home. On second thought, she wouldn't.

"Did Mother say scalawag? And backsides?" Nat whispered in my ear.

"She did."

"Why are you standing there gawking? We have work to do." Mama removed her bonnet, rolled up her sleeves, and started issuing orders. "Nathan, polish the furniture. Elizabeth, help Lois put fresh sheets on the beds. Morris, you and I shall commence with the kitchen. By the time the doctor arrives, I expect this house to sparkle."

And work we did.

Aunt Lois said, "Yes'm, Mistress Susan. Come along, Miss Elizabeth." She scurried up the stairs, amazingly lively for a lady her age. (Uncle Morris claims she's seventy. She admits nothing.)

"Mama would make a great general," I told Nat.

"Ladies do not …"

"…fight in wars. You said that already, but you are wrong. Women are …"

"Hush, children," Mama said. "I'll have no talk of war in my home. Go with Lois, Elizabeth. Get busy, Nathan."

An hour or so later, the house showed hardly a hint of damage, save for the holes in the wall, which were impossible to hide, though Mama tried by hanging paintings to cover them. Mama wiped her hands on her apron. "I'm pleased, children, Lois, Morris. The table is sturdy as ever, Nathan."

Despite her note of enthusiasm, I detected sadness in Mama's voice. "The house is beautiful," I said. It was, to me, no matter what others might think.

Nat added his own special touch in the form of a single red rose, probably the last flower in Vicksburg. It brought a smile to Mama's face. She put the rose in a crystal vase and set it on the table. "Perfect," she said. "Elizabeth, most of the china survived. We'll use the unbroken pieces for lunch. Nathan, fetch the silver from the sideboard. Our food may be tasteless, but our table shall be delightful. Your father must be content while he is home and not fret about the wounded, or us."

Mama's cheeks flushed as red as the rose. She lowered her lashes. "Excuse me now, children. I must change my dress and put a comb in my hair."

I watched her float up the stairs to make herself handsome for Papa. I had never realized how fond of him she was, or how brave she was to return to this house after our near tragedy last morning. Her love for Papa must be more powerful than her fear of the cannon.

"Lizzie, why is Mother's face red?" Nat asked. "Is she sick?"

"Sick?" I laughed. "She's in love."

He tugged at his ear, thinking. Suddenly his eyes lit up. "With Father."

"Who else? Take care with the china, Nat. These were Grandmother's dishes. Mama will take a willow switch to us if we break any more of them."

My concern was not necessary. Nat's hands were light, sure. The table was set, and we were arranging the silverware when Papa strode in. I flung myself at him. "Papa!"

He swept me up in his strong arms. Nat hung back, but Papa reached out and folded him close. "Look at you, Nathan," he said. "You've sprouted up overnight."

Nat's grin matched Papa's. "Yes, Father. One day I'll be as tall as you."

"Most likely." Papa held me out for a thorough inspection. "Elizabeth, you get prettier every day. Like your mother." He glanced around. "Where is she?"

"Upstairs," I said.

Papa kissed me on the nose, squeezed Nat's shoulder, and hurried off to find her.

"One of your fresh salads would be nice for lunch, Elizabeth," he called back.

ಬಃಬಃ

But all that was left of the radishes, onions, and peas Nat and I had planted in rows to spell out our names was a slice of earth plowed up by mortar shells and one or two wilted leaves of lettuce. I shook my fist at the gunboats on the river and shouted, "If you think destroying our gardens will starve us out, you're in for a big surprise, Yankees. We'll eat grass if we have to, weeds, but we will never surrender. We will win."

As though in answer, the sleeping mortars came to life. A shell burst above me, sending a shower of fire spiraling downward. One fell to my right, another to my left. I slapped my hands over my head and stood there, my feet rooted to the spot.

Nat appeared around the corner of the house and hustled me under the fig tree. "Get down, Lizzie," he said, his whole body shaking, but no more than mine.

I pried at his fingers to free myself. "I'm not afraid," I said.

He held me tightly. "I am."

Then Papa was there, shielding us with his body. For some reason, I had to explain about the salad. My words muffled against his chest I said, "The garden's gone, Papa."

I had not the slightest idea why that was important. I think it was because it meant the Yankees were in control. Because of them I could not make my father a simple salad. "Why don't the Yankees leave us alone, Papa? Why don't they go home?"

"You'd have to ask them, Elizabeth. Perhaps they believe what they're fighting for is right, the way we believe we are."

I lifted my face. "How can you defend them, Papa? We are right."

"I thought we were, once. Now ... I wonder if it matters. Every day I see young men, some no older than Nathan—he drew Nat closer—maimed, dying, before they've even lived. I just want it over. I want Willie and Joseph home."

His words faltered. "I ought to have stopped them," he said, more to himself than to Nat and me.

I recalled how Willie had gone off for the adventure, the excitement. Joseph went less willingly, torn between his desire to keep our nation whole and his need to protect his brother. Joseph was peace loving, like Nat. I could not see him in battle, harming a soul, even a Yankee. Willie was fearless, daring, impulsive, but he would never take a life. So why had they volunteered? For the same reason I was about to enlist. We all shared that Stamford code of honor: to defend the family, whatever the cost. "You could not stop them, Papa," I said.

No more than you can stop me, I added to myself.

઼ભ

After Mama and Papa retired to their room that afternoon to rest, I settled at the desk in the library to pen Joseph a letter. I had heard last from my brothers not long before the battle at Chancellorsville in early May. Many casualties occurred in that battle. I prayed they were not among the wounded. Perhaps the Yankees had intercepted the mail, and Joseph and Willie had not received my dispatches, or I theirs. I was a little anxious. Though Mama tried to hide her feelings, I could tell she was disturbed, as well. I had pulled pen and paper from the desk drawer and started my letter when Nat strolled over and deposited a strange-looking piece of wood in front of me.

"What's this?" I asked.

"What does it look like?"

I turned the wood over in my palm. I turned it sideways, upside down. I inspected the bottom and the top. If I called it the wrong thing, Nat would be crushed. I was almost certain I was correct when I said, "It looks like the gunboats on the river."

Nat raised his eyes to the ceiling, as if I were completely hopeless. "It's a flying machine, Lizzie."

"A machine that flies?"

He rolled his eyes at my ignorance. He pronounced each word carefully, for my inadequate comprehension, I suppose. "You should read something besides your poetry, Lizzie. Men have flown in balloon-shaped machines, filled with hot air. Years before they did this, the artist Leonardo da Vinci made drawings of flying machines. His pictures gave me the idea."

It was my turn to roll my eyes. I reached out, pressed the back of my hand to his forehead. "You're delirious, Nat. I'll call Papa to give you a dose of medicine to cure your vivid imagination."

"I explained my idea to Father."

I was more than curious. "What did he say?"

"He thinks I'm creative. He's heard of such machines, but he'll stay on the ground, just the same. You know what else?"

Flying machines indeed. "I haven't time for your nonsense, Nat." I proceeded to write my letter, but when my brother started something, he wouldn't rest until he finished it.

Nat turned my face to him. "When I build my flying machine, I'm going to travel to the moon and stars."

My pen scraped across the paper, leaving a splatter of ink. "The moon? Stars?" My short phrases and incomplete sentences sounded like a two-year-old learning to speak. But I was at a disadvantage. The moon was ... out there. We were ... here. I was at a loss to imagine what he meant. I blotted up the ink. Then I made the mistake of asking Nat his favorite question, "How?" which started him on a tidal wave of explanation.

"Think about it, Lizzie. We sail in ships on the rivers. A boat called a submarine goes under the water. We ride trains and carriages on land. Why can we not travel in air? I've read about men who are experimenting with this very idea. I plan to add my own invention."

Nat's explanation made sense. "Birds fly," I said, pleased with my observation. "Why not people?"

I could think of a million reasons, but Nat would have an argument for each of them. I examined the sculpture more closely. "It has wings like a bird."

"It does."

"So if we ride in your machine we can fly?"

"We can."

I did not credit all he said, but I dared not tell Nat. More than likely he was right. He read everything he could get his hands on about our earth, the oceans, and the heavens. I preferred Elizabeth Barrett Browning's poetry or Jane Austen's novels.

"You go ahead and fly, Nat. I'll keep my feet on the earth, with Papa."

Nat pulled a wing-backed chair to the desk. "You'll change your mind when you see it, Lizzie. May I have paper? There are some details I need help with, and Joseph is an artist. I'll ask him to draw a sketch of his ideas. We'll build it together."

"He'll like that." I gave Nat writing materials then commenced with my letter:

Vicksburg, Mississippi
Friday, May 22, 1863

Dearest Brother Joseph,

I pray you are well. Papa came home today for a rest. New lines appear on his face and dark circles surround his eyes. He is tired. I wish he would stay, but he won't. I wish ... Never mind.

Ammunition is scarce for our soldiers, like everything else. In order to save what they do have, our men fire only when necessary. Mama and the other women make cartridges, which helps some, but they cannot make percussion caps, which are in desperate need. Reports say that some are on the way. The courier had better have a fast horse.

We know not how long this siege will last, or if we shall live to see a new day. We pray that General Johnston's reinforcements will arrive soon. Then we'll see how brave the Yankees truly are.

Joseph, there's something I must know. Why did the army send your regiment away when we need you here in Vicksburg? Does General Lee not realize we are under siege? Perhaps you can explain. No one else can, not even Papa.

I have a secret to share with you By the time you read this, I shall be a Confederate soldier.

The click of boots on the polished wooden floor made me glance up in time to see Papa's huge figure fill the doorway. I put down my pen. The moment he walked into the library, I knew something was wrong.

Chapter 4

Papa's back was bent, like an old man's. A film of weariness clouded his eyes. He pushed his fingers against his temples. "Elizabeth, Nathan, a courier just rode over with a dispatch for me," he said. "More wounded have been brought to the hospital. I must go at once."

He was leaving! Already! No! He couldn't. Why did Nat and I have to sacrifice our father for men who had nothing better to do than fight each other? I had had enough. They were not taking my papa away again. I bolted to my feet and seized the sleeve of his jacket. "You just got here, Papa. We haven't sung around the piano, or walked in the garden, or played chess, or …"

He put a finger to my lips. "I know you're disappointed, Elizabeth. So am I. But I cannot ignore my duty to the wounded. I'll make it up to you the next time I'm home."

I pushed out my lower lip. "You always say next time."

"I regret having to shorten my visit, Elizabeth, especially after seeing the house and realizing the mortars make no distinction between soldiers and innocent citizens. Your mother tried to hide the damage to spare me, but I'm not blind."

"Is that not proof then that we need you more than the hospital does?"

He pinched the bridge of his nose between his thumb and finger. "This may seem contradictory to you, Elizabeth, and perhaps it is, but when I became a surgeon I made certain commitments. I also made promises to your mother when we married. Now I have to weigh one against the other. We have many casualties but few doctors. Your mother has courage and her children. She agrees with my decision to return."

"So you desert your family for … strangers."

The minute the words left my mouth, I realized how selfish I sounded. But I was tired of sharing my father. I fancied him all to myself, for a few days at least. Was that asking too much?

Gently he moved my hand. "This is not like you, Elizabeth. You're usually sensitive to the needs of others."

His troubled face made me feel two inches tall. My lower lip quivered, but I would have my say. "I do care about others, Papa. I care about us, too, even if you don't."

I shrank another inch.

Papa held my face between his big hands. "You and your mother and brother are more important to me than my own life, Elizabeth. I'll provide for you the best I can. But I must go. Send me a message by Morris should a crisis arise. I'll come at once."

"Will you?"

I sank as low as I could.

He sighed, released me. He reached inside his pocket, retrieved a gold locket, and snapped it around my neck. "This is your mother's, Elizabeth. Our family portrait is inside. When I've had an especially bad day, I look at it to remind me of my blessings. I want you to do the same."

I trailed a finger over the daguerreotype. Although the picture was tiny, the faces were clear. I would wear it close to my heart; but a locket was a poor substitute for my father.

Papa stroked his neatly trimmed, reddish-blond whiskers thoughtfully. "Since the house obviously is within range of the mortar shells and cannon, I'll see you, Nathan, and your mother to the cave before I depart."

The cave again? Papa had lost his mind, the same as Mama.

"We can't leave the house unprotected," I said in protest. "The Yankees are ruffians and thieves who'll steal everything they please."

"The house and furniture can be replaced, Elizabeth. You and your brother cannot. I'm uneasy about you. Promise me you'll listen to Nathan and your mother and do as they say."

Papa's brown eyes peered into my very soul. When I made a promise I kept it, the reason I made very few. And the reason I would never promise now.

He shook me gently but firmly. "Elizabeth, did you hear me?"

Nat whispered, "Promise, Lizzie."

How could I, when I would soon break it? I had lied to Mama once. I preferred not to add another to my already guilty conscience.

"What is the matter with you, Elizabeth?" Papa asked, sounding impatient.

I contemplated his every word. He had said "listen" to Nat and Mama. Not do. Just listen. So, interpreting his request in my own way, I said, "I promise to listen, Papa."

The minute I said, "I promise," a funny thing happened. A mixture of emotions crossed Papa's face, as if a heavy burden had been lifted from his shoulders. Somehow, the weight of those two words shifted from Papa to me. Saying them made me responsible.

When Nat added, "Lizzie keeps her promises," a tiny stab of guilt gnawed at my stomach. Why did he have to say that?

ഇൽ

All too soon we were at the cave, repeating more good-byes. Lately we'd had one farewell after another: First, my best friend, Miriam, and her family left Vicksburg, weeks ago, after a battle between Admiral David Porter's gunboats and our batteries. Willie, Joseph, and Patrick—whom I secretly loved—went next. Now Papa, for the hundredth time at least, was departing.

Mama buttoned his frock coat. With his handkerchief, Papa wiped a tear that clung to her eyelash. "I am sorry, Susan, to ruin our pleasant evening."

"Save your apologies, Charles," Mama said. "You are as dedicated to your profession as you are to your family, one of the reasons I love you. I would not have you any other way. The children and I shall manage."

"You know how to reach me, should you need anything," Papa said.

She kissed him. "Send those young men home, Charles, well and whole. Bring yourself back."

"As soon as possible."

I admired Mama's strength. I only hoped I was as brave, when the time came.

Papa turned to Nat. "Watch over your mother and sister, Son."

Nat's face was a sickly shade of gray at the responsibility Papa placed on his young shoulders. He answered with a boldness that did not quite reach his eyes. "I will, Father."

Papa kissed me on the nose, offering me a look of such trust that I lowered my eyes, afraid he'd read the truth in them.

Chapter 5

A FTER PAPA WAS GONE, Mama busied herself making the cave our home, a hopeless task. Home and cave go together like a bumblebee in a lady's bonnet. Even though Papa had brought as many of Mama's things from the house as would fit inside, a cave was a cave. Nothing in the whole state of Mississippi could make it our home. Try to convince Mama of that, however.

As usual—I would never learn—I had to speak my mind. "Great Granny's pantalets! You expect us to perform a miracle and turn this wretched cave into a comfortable home? I never heard anything so absurd."

The corners of Mama's mouth twitched down. "Mind your tongue, Elizabeth."

"Dirt walls," I said, so caught up in my misery I let her warning pass. "Dirt ceiling. Ugly, squiggling varmints too horrid to mention lurk beneath every clod of that dirt."

Mama swiped her hands on her apron. Her lips softened. "With a bit of imagination, we'll turn this um ... place into pleasant living quarters. Let me show you. Nathan, hang the portrait of you children on this wall." She indicated one of the wooden posts that braced the ceiling. "When you finish there, put the mirror in my room."

I crossed my arms over my bosom. "Why bother? Dust will cover the painting, like everything else. And it's too dark to see yourself in the mirror."

"Pshaw!" Mama said, dismissing my list of grievances. "We'll light our candle when necessary, Elizabeth, as well as the oil lamp your father brought, even though he says the glow shows the Yankees our location. We'll cover the entrance with a blanket. It's not so bad, honey. Now stop complaining and make yourself useful. Put down the strips of carpet. They'll keep the dampness of the floor from our feet."

"Carpet in a hole in the ground," I grumbled as I spread them out. "People living in caves. Next we'll be inviting the Yankees to take lunch with us. They'll certainly have a laugh to see the circumstances we're living in."

Mama set her workbox on the small table beside her rocking chair. "Remember, honey, this war is only temporary. One day our lives will return to normal."

Her eyes grew misty and her expression dreamy. "We shall have parties and friends over for tea. I'll make you a new gown out of that lovely green silk that matches your eyes. In fact, we'll celebrate your fifteenth birthday with a party. We'll invite all your friends. We'll have Lois bake a magnificent cake."

I tried to feel her excitement, but the cave was all around me. Shells rumbled and jarred the earth, reminders that our lives were anything but normal. Still, I could not help but recall how it was, before the Yankees came. Almost everyone in town came to Mama's parties. Although Nat and I were too young to attend, we'd sneak downstairs to listen to the music and watch the couples dance, the ladies' silk and lace dresses swirling in circles, the men looking dashing in their fancy clothes.

For a moment, music and laughter rang in my ears. The soft fabric of my new gown brushed my skin. Patrick, tall and dark, twirled me around the dance floor. I almost believed it could happen. Then a shell exploded. Dirt sifted down from the ceiling, reminding me of the truth. Cakes and parties were long ago. Life today was one big uncertainty. Tomorrow … God only knew if there was one. All I knew for certain was that Patrick would never dance with me. He'd never hold my hand or take me for long walks.

I looked at Nat, hanging the portrait. If this war lasted much longer, would he eventually be a part of it? My determination to enlist in the army grew stronger. Whether or not my participation would shorten the conflict, it would keep Nat at home, instead of going off like Willie and Joseph. He would never leave Mama alone.

As if realizing that more practical matters than parties had to be dealt with, Mama turned her attention to Nat. "Did you remember to bring clean stockings and unmentionables?"

Nat grunted, self-conscious at the mention of his drawers. He was so easy to tease that I couldn't resist. I held up his unmentionables. "He did," I said. "He also brought extra breeches and shirts."

I positioned a pair of his pants to my front. "How do I look?"

Nat glanced at me out of the corner of his eyes. "Like a girl. How else?"

Girl indeed. He had no imagination, save where his ships and stars and moon were concerned. I surveyed my reflection in the mirror leaning against the wall. I looked like a girl, of course, with my hair down to my waist. Something Nat had said earlier formed in my mind: Girls were not allowed in the army. I was aware of that. Most of the women who had enlisted had posed as men. Oftentimes they were discovered, but sometimes they were not. I swiveled from side to side, giving myself a closer look. If I wore Nat's pants and changed my hair, might I pass for a man? An interesting thought.

Later, Nat and Uncle Morris went out to gather firewood for supper. Since Aunt Lois was busy at the outdoor fireplace, and Mama was visiting our neighbors in a nearby cave, I decided to take advantage of my rare time alone to see if I might make a reasonable looking man. I slipped out of my dress and into Nat's shirt. His pants came next. Then I peered in the mirror and frowned. I looked not as manly as I had hoped. More like a little girl playing in her brother's clothes. A few alterations were necessary. Rolled up shirtsleeves, turned up hems, and a couple of my stockings tied together and wrapped around my middle for a belt, and my transformation, though less than perfect, was sufficient. I resembled a man, mostly, save for one minor detail.

I curled a strand of hair around my hand. Willie thought my hair was magnificent. Mama brushed it for hours to make it soft and shimmery. Papa and Joseph quietly approved. Nat wasn't one to offer compliments, but he would not fancy it short. For me to be a man, though, the hair had to go. I picked up Mama's scissors. I tossed them down. Was such a drastic step really necessary? I searched my brain, came up with nothing better. Which was more important, my hair or Vicksburg? I was quite fond of my hair, but I loved my city, my home.

"Stop being wishy-washy," I scolded myself. I snatched up Mama's scissors, flung them down. A long minute dragged by. I looked at those shiny scissors in Mama's workbox, daring me. I had to make up my mind, one way or the other. "It's only hair, Lizzie. Do it quickly, like swallowing a spoonful of medicine. Then it won't hurt so much."

I grabbed the scissors and snipped off a wisp. Brown hair floated to the floor. "See. Perfectly painless."

Braver now. Another snip. More hair feathered at my feet. Who was I trying to convince? It wasn't painless after all. In fact, it hurt quite a bit, not physically, but in my mind. I dropped the scissors like hotcakes and studied my reflection in the mirror. I smoothed my hair over the bare place. Was I so vain as to consider my hair more important than my home and family? There must be an easier way. Nat would have an answer. If only I could ask him, he'd say, "Silly girl. There is."

I felt a smile curl at the corners of my mouth. In minutes I had braided my hair and piled it on top of my head. One more part to my disguise, and I was ready. I plunked Nat's cap on my head and viewed myself in the mirror. A young boy gazed back. A brown tangle peeked from under the cap. I shoved it in and fancied myself taller and heavier. I wasn't, but I could change only so much. Nonetheless, by tomorrow, if all went according to plan, I would be a Confederate soldier in General John Pemberton's army.

A little voice inside me said, "You promised, Lizzie."

"I did not promise to live in the cave," I snapped in annoyance. "I did not promise not to enlist in the army. I promised to listen to

Nat and Mama. I listened. Now it's time to act. I am no longer Elizabeth Susan Stamford, only daughter of Charles and Susan."

The boy in the mirror arched an eyebrow in the fashion typical of Stamford men.

"Then who are you?" he asked.

"Just call me Eli."

Chapter 6

THAT EVENING MAMA SAT in her rocking chair, mending socks and sewing buttons from worn-out shirts onto still wearable ones. Buttons were scarce; thread was in short supply; paper, ink, and pens were impossible to procure, so we wasted nothing. If the siege lasted for a time, I'd have to turn the pages of my letters sideways and write across the words. Or write with pencil for my brothers to erase and use the paper again. But I would write.

While Mama sewed, I strummed my guitar. With my departure only hours away, I found myself memorizing every line of her nose and lips and eyes, every hair on her head, the curve of her neck, her delicate hands. Soon I'd be on my own, no mother to calm my fears, to offer advice, to remind me to act like a lady. I moved closer and settled on the floor in front of her, for the time we had left together.

Mama laid her mending on the table, gave me a wistful look. "Elizabeth—"

"'Home Sweet Home?'" I asked.

"How did you know?"

"I have a need to hear it, too."

I played, and Mama hummed along. From without the cave's entrance where he was looking through his telescope, Nat's voice rang out. Poor Nat. He didn't realize he sounded worse than the braying of a sick mule. Since I had not the heart to tell him, I plucked the strings harder, in an attempt to drown out his voice. But the louder I played, the louder he sang. How could he sound so dreadful? Willie had the voice of an angel. Joseph was fair. Me? Don't even ask. I provided the guitar or piano accompaniment. When I did sing, on occasion, Mama's face puckered in a pained expression, as though she had stubbed her toe. I wasn't as bad as

Nat, but close. We managed to conclude the song without so much as a giggle from Mama or me. Nat was blissfully unaware.

Mama beckoned him to her side. "Have I told you how thankful I am that you and Elizabeth are safe with me, Nathan? Mrs. Lance's four sons fought in the battle at Champion Hill, when it fell to General Grant and his army. She has received no word from them since, but keeps her faith by believing they are in Vicksburg and will call on her soon."

"Oh, not the Lance brothers!" I cried.

I knew them well. Along with Willie, they were always in some mischief or other. I rested my head in Mama's lap. For the longest time, no one spoke. We were each lost in our own thoughts. Distant sounds carried on the wind. Yankee voices. Voices with the slow, southern drawl, talking friendly-like. Although they were too far away to hear clearly, a stray word now and then reached my ears. One man asked about his son, who apparently was in our army. An excited "Pa? Is that you?" replied.

"Father and son," Mama said softly, "meeting each other in the most unexpected place. How lovely."

Unlike Mama, who seemed not to realize they most likely were on opposite sides, I thought it tragic. Would the father kill his own flesh and blood? Would the son? That's another thing I hate about this war. It destroys family loyalties. Forces brother against brother. Father against son. At least my brothers and I share the same beliefs. If we meet on the battlefield, we shall fight side by side.

That all too familiar pinch of guilt rippled through me. I raised my head. I suppose I wanted Mama's approval when I asked, "If a person believes he or she has to do something, even though others tell her or him he's wrong, is he? Wrong, I mean?"

Like Nat, Mama seldom rushed into anything. Save when her children's lives were in danger, I reminded myself, recalling the shell that had lodged itself above my bed. She had moved with haste then. I waited, but she did not seem inclined to answer. "Is he?" I asked impatiently.

"You've asked a difficult question, honey." Mama tucked her lower lip under her teeth, thinking. "It depends," she said. "We all must do what we believe is best. Sometimes we're wrong, but whatever decisions we make, we must be prepared to live with them. So rather than do something we'll regret later, we ought to think the matter through carefully and consider the consequences of our actions, both good and bad."

"Like Willie and Joseph did?"

A wrinkle appeared between Mama's eyes. "I seriously doubt your brothers thought about the repercussions of their impulsive deed when they enlisted in the army. I pray they have no regrets now. Remember, honey, what each of us does affects not only us, but the rest of the family as well. Once a decision is made, one rarely has the opportunity to go back and change it."

"Like Willie and Joseph," I said again. "Our family is only half a family without them."

Mama's wrinkle line deepened. "Elizabeth honey, do you have anything you wish to tell me?"

I contemplated that a moment. Mama had told me exactly what I needed to hear. I was at peace with my decision. For better or worse, I had made my choice. I shook my head. "Just thank you, Mama."

"May I ask then what happened to your hair?"

Mama's eyes were as sharp as an owl's. I cast about in my mind for a sensible explanation. "My hair was ... tangled." That was true. "I only meant to trim a little." Just enough to look like a man. "Somehow, the scissors slipped." I offered her hope. "It will grow back."

Mama fingered my hair. She sighed. "So it will." She gave me a quizzical smile. "Honey, is your hair the reason you asked me about making decisions?"

Mama thought ... My breath rushed out. I hadn't even realized I was holding it. "Partly," I said.

Mama swatted at a mosquito, buzzing her ear. "What a mess our lives have become. How I wish your father were here. Then we'd not be battling these pesky insects that are determined to have us for supper. I swear he cares more for his injured men than he does for his family. Whenever an emergency arises, he races off to that hospital, leaving us with no protection. How is a person supposed to breathe in this stuffy, dusty hole? How are ..."

Mama turned her face away. "Here I am complaining after I scolded you for doing the same. Your father would be shocked to hear me running on so."

She turned back. "Honey, you are charming and intelligent, a delight to your father and me, but you are also headstrong, inquisitive, and impulsive, not the most desirable traits in a young lady. You must be gentle, soft-spoken, and agreeable, Elizabeth. Then the proper decisions will come easy."

Proper decisions? After fourteen years, she ought to know me better. After fourteen years of having this almost identical conversation, too many times to count, I ought to learn to keep my mouth quiet. But this time was different. This was not about dresses, or manners, or whether I lowered my lashes and pretended shyness to attract a beau. This was about me, about who I am. "I have to be myself," I said.

Mama pursed her lips. Her fan whipped faster than a hummingbird's wings. "With your attitude and manners, Elizabeth, or rather lack of them, no suitable young gentleman will fancy marrying you."

At the present, suitable young gentlemen were the last thing on my mind. Even so, I could not help but remind Mama that she had gone against her mother and father's wishes on more than one occasion. "Oh? Did Papa marry you because you were the proper lady? Did Grandfather and Grandmother pick him for you? Or did you ignore them and choose the man you loved, regardless of their opinions?"

Mama had no argument there. They had not. I knew the story backward and forward and treasured every word of it. Mama's parents were opposed to her choice of the handsome young fellow from New York. Although he had worked hard to graduate from medical school and had a bright future as a surgeon, he was poor. He was beneath Mama socially. Half the young men in Vicksburg courted her, but she refused them all, for Charles Stamford. When her parents forbade Mama to see the dashing young Northerner, he stole her away. For months after they married, her family would not see or speak to their only daughter. Only when Joseph was born did they relent and forgive her. My hope was that Mama and Papa would recall how they had felt without her family's love, and forgive me when I enlisted in the army. Perhaps not right away, but one day.

Although she hid her face with her fan, I saw the slightest trace of a smile. "I never should have told you that story, Elizabeth. Seriously, honey, we have to trust those who love us and know what is best. We also have to trust our heart," she added softly.

I touched her arm. "I'm glad you did the last. I like Papa for my father."

Later, when Mama was sleeping, I left a note on her pillow:

Dearest Mama,

My heart speaks plain and true. I plan to join General Pemberton's army. It is a matter of pride and honor. I will write.

Say a prayer for me.
Love you always, Lizzie

Chapter 7

ONCE AGAIN NAT SEEMED DESTINED to ruin my plans. I easily slipped past Aunt Lois and Uncle Morris, fast asleep, but I practically tripped over Nat, sitting without the entrance of the cave, gazing through his telescope at the starry sky. I had not heard a peep out of him and thought he was sleeping.

He looked up, as if expecting me. "You want to see the North Star, Lizzie?"

Biting my lower lip to hold back the "not especially" that threatened to pour forth from my mouth, I sat myself on the ground beside him. I wasn't angry with Nat. I was the one at fault for not planning better. All wasn't lost, however. He'd fall asleep before long. I could wait.

He angled the telescope my way.

The sparkling lights all looked the same to me. "Which one is it?"

"The bright one. There." He tilted my head in the right direction. "The North Star, also known as Polaris, is part of the Little Bear constellation, or Ursa Minor. It's at the tip of the handle of the part called The Little Dipper. Sailors use the North Star to guide them when they're far out to sea, along with a compass."

"When I need a star to guide me, I'll remember that."

Careful to keep Nat's pants and shirt concealed in my crinoline, I stretched out on the grass. The night was fairly quiet, after the heavy bombardment we'd heard continually this day. We know not what the morrow will bring. More of the same, I suppose. And I shall be in the midst of it.

Nat explored my face, his eyebrows raised. "You promised, Lizzie," he said.

That's another thing about my brother. His memory is perfect. He recalls every little thing I say or do, whether now or long ago.

The way I used to rock him when he was a baby, even though he was almost as big as me. The hours we spent exploring the woods. Nat could name every plant and animal we encountered. We had always been close. For that reason, Nat was the hardest to leave.

"Don't run away, Lizzie."

My throat tightened. Why was he making this so difficult? I had thought it would be easy, but I was wrong. Unable to look him in the eyes, I rolled onto my side, my back to him. "I won't run away," I said.

I wouldn't. A girl who runs away doesn't know where she's going. I know.

I lay very quietly, so quietly that Nat leaned over me. "Lizzie?"

He believed I was asleep, and he relaxed. I soon heard his slow, even breathing.

"Nat," I said to make sure.

Silence.

I waited awhile longer and then cautiously arose. A twig snapped under my foot, but Nat was lost in his world of dreams and flying machines and traveling to the stars. In the square of moonlight, his face glowed, sweet and innocent. With one final look, to impress his gentle face in my memory, I snatched up my skirt and ran. When I had crossed the ravine and was out of sight of the cave, I hid behind a giant oak tree and shrugged out of my dress and crinoline.

As I stood there in my ruffled pantalets, unfolding Nat's trousers and shirt, an odd sensation that I was not alone came over me. I backed against the rough bark of the tree and squinted into the darkness. I saw nothing, but heard the bushes to my right rustle. Heavy footsteps clumped toward me. I clutched the clothes to my chest. My legs knocked together louder than the beat of a drum. What should I do? Run? Hide? Scream? They all sounded reasonable.

Suddenly, a huge shape broke through the trees, not ten feet distant. I yelped, buried my face in the clothes, my eyes squeezed shut, and prayed whoever was there was blind, or I was invisible, or a tree branch would strike him on the head. My prayers went unanswered, for the steps thumped closer. It was too late to run, so I drew in my breath and willed the intruder to pass by without seeing me.

"Moo."

Moo? In spite of my fears, my eyes sprang open. My heart beat faster than a galloping horse, as I stared into dark, liquid eyes, staring back at me.

A cow. My eyes blurred with tears. A stupid cow. So close I could touch her. Tears switched to near hysterical giggles then back to tears. My knees were so weak I had to sit down. Gradually, my heartbeat slowed. My senses returned. I wiped my eyes with the back of my arm. What would Willie and Joseph think if they saw me afraid of a cow? Willie would tease me unmercifully. Joseph would say nothing, but he'd think me a coward. Well, I wasn't. I lifted my chin and managed to laugh at my silly self.

"You're just a cow," I told the animal. "A harmless cow."

The cow lowered her head and nibbled the grass, and I thought how good she would taste. Some hungry family would have her for supper. I hoped she wasn't the neighbor's cow where Uncle Morris got our milk. I started to take her to him, but I had delayed too long already. Putting the encounter with the cow behind me, I proceeded to turn myself into a man. I would not have to wear Nat's trousers for long. Once I was in the army, they'd issue me a uniform, and I would truly be a soldier. I piled my hair on top of my head, added Nat's cap, and pushed it forward. In my most solemn voice I said, "General Pemberton, I'm called Eli. I've come to enlist in your army."

Great Granny's pantalets! My outward appearance might fool the general, but my voice was definitely that of a girl. On second thought, General Pemberton would recognize me anyway, even in disguise. He had taken tea at our house on several occasions. He had dined with us at supper. I could not risk him notifying Papa. I'd have to find another officer, one who was not familiar with my family, or me. Or I might not need an officer. I might just blend in with the other soldiers, pretend I was one of them. I imagine new volunteers come and go all the time. No one would pay attention to one more.

Satisfied with this strategy, I concealed my dress behind some bushes and marched toward the rifle pits, and, hopefully, the Confederate lines. I had heard the Yankees were dug in very close to our trenches. One wrong step and I'd end up a prisoner, rather than a soldier. On the way, I practiced a deeper voice. "I'm called Eli."

In the dusky field ahead, something moved. I halted. White moonlight beamed down on a large, hulking figure, leaning over a lump on the ground. A second figure prowled off to the side. Bending. Rising. Bending. They were not lost cows. I had not expected to see anyone this soon. I must be closer to the entrenchments than I thought.

Voices glided through the breathless air, which was as still as I was.

"Found us another rifle, Bruin," a soft voice said, "and some cartridges."

A crackled, rusty voice replied, "I got a gold watch, Arnold. A deck of cards. Tobacco."

Soldiers! What were they talking about? Where were they getting these items? In the twinkle of starlight, I strained to see whether they were Yankees or our boys. Their voices were slow and smooth, southern like, but I was uncertain. It occurred to me that they would not know which side I was on either. Since the possibility existed they'd mistake me for the enemy and shoot me on sight, I dropped flat to the ground and found myself face-to-face with blank eyes, gaping at the heavens, seeing nothing. A scream gurgled in my throat. I clapped my hand over my mouth, bit my lip, tasted blood.

My other hand touched something wet and sticky. The scream tore loose. I couldn't stop it.

The men turned.

Words I had never heard spewed forth from rusty voice Bruin's mouth. "Peers we've got us a live one, Arnold," he said.

"Let's see if we can help him," Arnold said.

Bruin laughed. "A bayonet in his gut should help him right out of his misery."

Chills scooted up one side of my body and down the other. I burrowed deeper, mashing my face into the earth. Play dead, Lizzie, I told myself. It's your only chance. Lie still. The grass crunched under the thud of boots. I clenched my fists so tightly my fingernails dug into my flesh. I scarcely felt the pain.

Then something hard prodded me in the side. A rough hand grasped my shoulder and yanked me over. Another shriek ripped from the bottom of my soul, froze on my lips at the sight of a musket aimed right at my nose.

Chapter 8

AN UGLY, WHISKERED FACE GLOWERED at me from the other end of the musket. He was going to shoot me. Here. Now. No one would know what happened to me. Not Mama. Or Papa. Or Nat. Bubbles of perspiration dripped down my neck. Nausea rose in my throat. I opened my mouth to plead for my life, but no sound came out.

The other man bent over me. "Aw, he's just a boy, Bruin, no more than twelve. You can't shoot a boy."

"I can if he's a Yank," Bruin said.

Yank? Then they were … I blinked dirt and grass out of my eyes and took a closer look. Gray. Their uniforms were gray. I breathed a little easier, though not much, so long as that musket stared me in the eye. "Y-you're Confederate?" I stammered in a squeaky voice that bore little resemblance to mine.

"Reckon we are," Bruin said. "Who in tarnation might you be?"

Why was he talking to me as if I were the enemy? Did he not know? Of course not. I wasn't dressed in gray. For all he knew I was a Yankee. Fear curled in my stomach. I gulped. "I … I'm on your s-side," I said.

"Hear that, Arnold?" Bruin said. "Boy here says he's one of us."

"It don't matter which side you're on, son," Arnold said. His face was round and kind. "What're you doin' out here?"

Bruin raised the musket, balanced it on his shoulder. "Well, speak up, boy!"

Now that I wasn't facing that glint of metal, I summoned what little courage I had, which was very little at the moment, and stood up. I brushed my sticky hand on my trousers and quickly tucked a straggle of wild hair under my cap. Speak in low voice, I reminded myself. "I wish to join your regiment," I said, hardly stuttering at all.

Bruin guffawed and slapped his knee. "Would ya listen to that. Boy wants to be a soldier."

He was making fun of me. Arnold was watching me, an unreadable expression on his face. If I couldn't fool these two men, I'd never become a soldier. I shoved my hands in my trouser pockets to keep them from shaking.

Arnold narrowed his eyes. "You're a mite young to join the army, son."

"I'm near sixteen."

I only stretched my age a bit more than a year. Whether he suspected I was lying or not, he never admitted it. I liked this Arnold fellow.

"My son's twelve," he said. "He's about your size. Huskier. It's been months since I last saw him."

"I have a brother, twelve."

"Do you now?" Arnold rubbed the back of his neck. "What's your name, son? Does your ma know where you are?"

I was amazed how natural Eli sounded, as though it were my birth name, when I said, "I'm called Eli. Mama ... my ma knows where I am."

Or she would once she read my note.

"Well, Eli, we can't leave you out here. Come with us. We'll see what we can do. I'm Private Arnold. This ornery fellow is Private Bruin. He ain't half as bad as he acts."

That was a matter of opinion.

"A fine fix our army's in when our men are scarce knee-high to a milk stool," Bruin said. He reached down, snagged the rifle off the dead man. "Since you're aimin' to fight, boy, a soldier's got to have a weapon. Catch." He tossed the rifle at me.

When I caught it, he gave another horselaugh. "Don't shoot off your own foot."

The Yankees could not be any more intimidating than Private Bruin was. Even so, I was determined to prove I'd make a good soldier. I lifted my head and straightened my back to my full height, which was considerably less than the private's. "I can shoot," I informed him, although I had never held a gun in my hands, not even Papa's Colt revolver. I would learn.

Private Bruin snorted. "You'll get your chance to prove it come morning, Eli, if not sooner."

I ran a hand over the smooth barrel of the musket and wondered if the man at my feet had a son or daughter, somewhere, waiting for the father who would never return. How would I feel if he were Papa? The very thought made me light-headed and dizzy. I could not bear it. Sad for the unknown casualty, sad for his family, I tramped across the field after Arnold and Bruin. With each victim I passed, whether clad in the blue or the gray, and there were many of both, a bitter taste soured my mouth. The smell of death hung in the night air. Everywhere I stepped there were lifeless bodies. Were the father and son who had been reunited among the casualties, their lips silenced, never to greet one another again? I prayed not.

As I crossed over one body, something latched onto my ankle. I slapped my hand over my mouth to stifle a whimper and glanced down. Long, bloody fingers were coiled around my leg. A soldier, his face shadowed, featureless, begged, "Help me."

Panic threatened. I longed to shake my leg free, to be rid of him. The starlight, for a second, revealed the soldier's eyes, imploring me to do something. I couldn't. I didn't know what. Or how. But what if he were Willie, or Joseph? I'd find a way to provide aid for them, would I not? So I should with this man. "How … how can I help?" I asked.

Private Arnold took one look, sighed, and shook his head. "Pray for him, Eli."

So I did.

Gagging at the stench of death, my stomach threatening to empty itself of its contents, I stayed close to Private Arnold and threaded my way through the fallen men. Finally, we hunkered down in the rifle pits. I was thankful everyone was too busy to pay much attention to me. It gave me time to compose myself. This was what I wanted, wasn't it? This was where I belonged. I scanned the soldiers around me, almost invisible in the night. From what I could see, they were filthy, and some had grimy bandages on arms or legs or heads. I had never beheld anything like it. Had I acted in haste, as Mama warned me against?

Someone handed me a Bible. Arnold and Bruin were not the only soldiers who had plucked souvenirs from the battlefield. The men were passing around rifles and cartridges, along with small trinkets, watches, playing cards, magazines, and books. Bruin gave me a box of cartridges. I knew what they were, but had not a single idea how to load them.

Arnold made no comment on my earlier boast that I had experience with guns. Instead, he gave me a quick lesson on how to pour the powder down the muzzle, push in the bullet, pull back the hammer, place the percussion cap under the hammer, aim, and squeeze the trigger. When I tried, however, most of my powder sifted to the ground. Arnold shared his with me.

After he loaded his own rifle he asked, "Was that the first dead man you've seen, Eli?"

I remembered to disguise my voice. "Yes, except for my grandparents. But they weren't covered with blood, and they seemed peaceful. How did you know?"

"Your face was green, even in the dark."

"Oh."

"It doesn't get any easier."

"That's what my brothers say. I wasn't sure what they meant. Until now."

The babble of voices dimmed, as exhausted soldiers sought rest. Private Arnold pulled his cap over his eyes and leaned back against the embankment. I huddled in the trench, the bloody faces, the torn and twisted bodies haunting me. I'd never sleep again. My body said otherwise.

The dawn brought with it gray clouds and the prospect of rain.

During the brief break in action that occurred most days at breakfast time, or so Arnold told me, I reached into the pocket of Nat's trousers and withdrew a scrap of paper and a pencil I remembered to bring, should the opportunity to write my brothers occur. The pencil was short, the paper small, so I'd better make each word count. I started the letter to Willie then decided to address it to Joseph, as well. I had to share my feelings of the horror I had witnessed. They would understand. They had seen it, too.

Vicksburg, Mississippi
Saturday, May 23, 1863

Dearest Brothers,

I take pen in hand to tell you that I've done it. Well, almost.

I'm not in the army officially, but I am in the trenches with the soldiers. I even have a rifle, lifted from the enemy killed in yesterday's battle. Private Arnold showed me how to fire it. Mama and Nat and I heard the fighting from the cave, but hearing and seeing are two different matters. Thousands of men on both sides were killed, I think, from the number of corpses I saw in the field.

The images flooded back, and my heart fluttered, making me feel faint. I swallowed hard to choke back the memories, but even when I returned to my letter, they were there, in the back of my mind. My writing was quite messy. I hoped they could read it.

What you once said, Willie, about war being ugly and nothing like you imagined is true. Last night, I witnessed death. I care not to see it again, but fear I shall. Tell me, brothers, why are we killing friend and neighbor and stranger? Some say it is to free the slaves.

I think there is more to it. Perhaps if I understood the reasons I could make some sense of this horror. What do you think, Joseph? Willie?

Rain is falling. Yankee cannon are firing. I hope their guns clog with water.

Love you always,
Eli (my new name)

P. S. To explain Eli: You see, I am a boy. Or so everyone believes.

Shells poured down like giant hailstones. Cold, stinging rain drenched us. Rifle fire cracked around us, sharpshooters taking target practice at any head that appeared above the parapet. Our guns responded. Between the thunder and the gunfire, the earth quaked. I picked up my rifle, balanced it on the breastworks, and pointed it at the puffs of smoke in the hills, where the Yankees were.

"Here, Eli, since you're now a soldier you need this." Private Arnold removed Nat's cap and replaced it with a gray forage cap. "I thought so," he whispered.

Even though he now knew I was a girl, he kept my secret. I liked him even more.

"Take careful aim, Eli," he said, his voice as gentle as Papa's. "Make every shot count. Keep your head down."

Those were the last words he spoke to me, or to anyone. I felt the breeze of something whine past my head. Without a sound, he slumped back. I shook his arm.

"Private Arnold!"

Rain mingled with blood. Rain mingled with tears. He had a son, just twelve years old, the same as Nat.

The gunboats hammered away. Muskets blazed. Shells hissed, exploded. I never fired a shot. I was too numb. The rain slowed, came to an end, and flies, droning, whirring, murmuring, crawled on Private Arnold. Unbearable pain gripped me. The pea bread I had eaten earlier rumbled. I was going to be sick. I scrambled up the embankment.

"Hey!" Private Bruin shouted. "Get down, Eli!"

He grabbed for me, but I broke free and fled to the shelter of the trees, where I dropped to my knees and vomited. Hugging my arms to me, I rocked back and forth, back and forth. Private Arnold's words, when he taught me how to use the rifle, when he told me about his son, swirled in my brain. I sobbed. I sniffled. I hiccupped. I longed for Mama's gentle arms around me, reassuring, promising everything would be all right. I longed for Papa to cradle me against his broad chest and call me his precious little honey.

I swiped the hem of Nat's shirt angrily at my shameful tears. What had I expected? That war was an afternoon tea party? Mama warned me. I did not listen. Even worse, I was a deserter, the vilest creature on earth, next to the Yankees. I had brought shame to my family. Perhaps it wasn't too late. If I hurried back, no one would know.

Quickly, before I had second thoughts, I got to my feet, turned, and for the second time in only a few hours found myself face-to-face with a rifle.

"Don't move, Reb."

Chapter 9

A SOLDIER, YANKEE, SPRAWLED on the ground, his back against a tree, a rifle held in his left hand, pointed at me. His right arm, bloody and mangled, hung uselessly at his side.

Instead of flinching with fear as I had done on the battlefield, something snapped in my brain. A rush of anger flared up in my very soul. I was tired of guns and war and Yankees. This despicable varmint quite possibly was the Yankee who had killed Private Arnold. If not, he surely had ended the lives of other brave Confederates. Any sense of sanity I once possessed flew away. Blinded by an uncontrollable rage I yelled, "Don't move or what? You'll shoot me, you contemptible, impertinent Yankee dog? Well, I have you in my sights, too."

Only then did I realize I had lost my musket somewhere between the trees and the trenches. A fine soldier I was, unable even to keep my weapon.

He did not shoot, however, for just then a gurgling wheeze seized his body. His head drooped to his chest, and the rifle slid from his hand. The rattling in his throat was the only sign that he still lived. Now was my chance to get his weapon and put an end to his miserable life. Cautiously, I reached down and took possession of the rifle. I mashed it against his head. "This is for Private Arnold," I said, "and all the others."

So why did I hesitate? Why did I not pull the trigger? I lowered the rifle. I could not kill a helpless man, even a Yankee. It wasn't necessary, anyway. Without medical care, he would die soon enough. The thought pleased me. After all, the Yankees were to blame for this insane war. Had they stayed at home and not invaded us, no one would have died. My brothers would be here. We'd be laughing and singing. I owed this soldier nothing, but I did owe myself. I had to return to the trenches and prove I wasn't a coward. I spun about, and, closing my ears to the groans of pain coming from behind me, trudged off. He was one less Yankee murderer to fear, one less soldier for Papa to attend to.

Papa. I halted. Why did I have to think of him? Papa would never leave a wounded soldier to die, no matter the color of his uniform. He would say the man has a mother, a father, children perhaps, brothers, sisters. I shook my head, folded my arms. "But I'm not Papa," I said, arguing with myself. "I don't know the first thing about treating battle wounds. He's a Yankee. No one will fault me for leaving him. Perhaps one of his own will find him."

"Perhaps not," said a reproving voice. "Do you wish to be responsible for his death, Lizzie? Besides, you've seen your father with his patients. You know what to do."

Reluctantly, I concluded I could no more abandon the injured soldier than Papa could. With a sigh of resignation, I padded back to the Yankee and stood there for a long while, unable to make up my mind what I should do next. Weak from loss of blood, he hardly moved. I had no medicine, nothing to ease his suffering. What was I to do? I glanced around, as though the answer would magically appear. We were in a thicket of trees out of the main line of battle, although an occasional stray bullet whistled past. He was in little danger of another shot finding him. He'd be all right until someone else came along. Besides, he was... bloody and smelly. I dared not touch him. I wasn't a doctor or a nurse. These were all good reasons to proceed on my way. Convinced I could do nothing, I turned, took a faltering step, but the thought of Willie or Joseph, sick or wounded on some distant field, surrounded by the enemy, drew me back. What I did now for this soldier, I prayed some caring soul would do for them.

I knelt and pulled back the Yankee's stained, mud-spattered shirt. Blood and yellowish-white pus oozed from a hole in his upper arm, just below the shoulder. How I choked back the vomit was a mystery, but I did. One thing I was sure of, he needed more care than I was able to provide.

"My father's a surgeon," I said, doubtful the soldier was clear-headed enough to comprehend. "I'll take you to the hospital."

He opened his eyes. "The hospital," I repeated.

I shall never forget the way he pleaded, "No... hospital. Don't... cut... off... arm."

"Nobody's going to cut off your arm, soldier."

But they might, I knew. I had heard Papa tell Mama, his voice thick with emotion. Would losing a limb be worse than dying? Imagine going through life with part of you missing. How dreadful to live so! Could I prevent that from happening to this Yankee? Why should I bother? He was the foe who was tearing my family and my life apart. My common sense told me he was dying and nothing I could do would save him. Another part of me argued that whether I succeeded or not, I had to try. Papa would. My brothers would.

"Lie still, soldier," I said. "I'll dress your wound to stop the bleeding, until we get to the hospital."

I pulled my shirt out of my trousers, tore a strip off the bottom, and wrapped his arm the way I had seen Papa do.

"Don't wanna... die... far from... home," he said, his glazed eyes tracking my every movement. Despite his obvious pain, he never cried out.

"My father's a good surgeon," was all I said. I could promise nothing.

"Thank...you," the Yankee said when the bandage was in place.

This Yankee had manners. Mama would not believe it. I considered this startling revelation only briefly, for I had the problem of how to remove him to the Confederate hospital, located in one of the residences about a quarter mile behind the lines, and not too distant from my house.

"Can you walk?" I asked him.

He pushed up, leaned against the tree. "I'll try. Why...."

Why was I helping him was his unfinished question. "For my brothers," I said.

He nodded.

I fashioned a sling for his arm, then we made our way out of the trees, his good arm over my shoulders, my arm around his waist. The Yankee drifted in and out of consciousness, yet his legs were fairly sturdy as slow step by slow step we crossed the field. Shells whizzed around us. We had to duck more than once to avoid losing our heads. We finally reached the street to my house. The hospital was two squares beyond. Such a forlorn picture the deserted houses painted. Scarcely a one had not suffered some injury. When the chimney of my house came into view, I hastened forward, anxious to see if it was whole. But the Yankee fell to the ground, almost dragging me with him.

"Rest. Please," he said.

Rest. I was tempted. He was heavy for a man not much taller than Nat, and thinner. My back ached from his weight. I even fiddled with the idea of abandoning him, rushing into my house, and locking myself in my room, until this war ended. The report of gunfire changed my mind. I suddenly yearned to see Mama, at the cave. And Nat. I had made a terrible mistake. I was not meant to be a soldier. I longed to be with my family. The sooner the Yankee was at the hospital, the sooner I could go home. I shoved my arm under his good shoulder and pulled him up.

"We're almost there," I said. "Then you can rest."

The street seemed to grow steeper with each step we took. I knew to go as far as the hospital was impossible. Even if I was able to continue, the Yankee was not. Dared I take him into my home? Mama would faint in shock at the idea of the enemy within our walls. My head throbbed with indecision. Mama wouldn't know. She rarely left the cave. By the time she decided to venture to the house the Yankee would be in the hospital or...

I waved that thought aside. "Come on, soldier. We'll rest at my house."

We had reached the front gate and were about to go in when I caught a glimpse of two gray-clad soldiers half a square down the

street. Confederates. Perfect. They would carry the Yankee to the
hospital for me. Intent on their conversation, the soldiers hadn't
seen us. I raised my arm to get their attention, let it fall. I think the
soldiers would not harm me, but the Yankee might be less fortunate. Why did I care? Again, my brothers. Since we couldn't reach
the house without the soldiers spotting us, I shoved the Yankee
behind the nearest hiding place, a hedge of azalea bushes, and dived
in after him.

He clutched his arm and groaned, "Oooh."

I clamped my hand over his mouth. "Quiet. Confederates."

Understanding, he crouched down. Pearls of moisture glistened
on his brow. Through the leaves I watched the soldiers approach.
Seconds later they were on the other side of the hedge.

"I'm positive I saw somebody," the squatty, round soldier said.

"You're just jumpy, Zeke," the other soldier said.

"Un-huh. They were standing here, John, plain as day. Two of
'em. One short, one taller. Couldn't tell whether they were Yanks or
Rebs. Check those bushes."

With the barrels of their muskets they bent back branches of the
azaleas. A little more to the right and they'd discover us. We were
defenseless, had no weapons. Unable to carry both the Yankee and
his rifle, I had discarded it back in the trees. No matter. I wouldn't
shoot a Confederate.

"I don't see anybody," John said.

"That's 'cause you're blinder than an old woman. They couldn't
have gotten far. Keep looking."

The Yankee moved restlessly. "Water," he whispered, but loud
enough to alert the Confederates.

"Here that," Zeke said. "They're in the hedge."

"Hey, we know you're there," John said. "Show yourselves."

The Yankee staggered to his feet. "Won't... let them... take...
me... alive. Where's... rifle?"

Were all Yankees so foolish? He stood little chance against the
two healthy soldiers. Why I kept helping him puzzled me. I loathed

him and all Yankees for what they had done, were doing. I ought to let the soldiers have him, but I had promised myself to fetch him to the hospital. A promise was a promise, and I had enough to answer for already. I put my hand on his arm.

"Stay here," I said, and scooted out of the azaleas, a plausible story forming in my mind.

"Were you speaking to me?" I asked in all innocence. I avoided looking at the muskets in their hands.

Both soldiers' eyes almost popped out of their heads. They clearly were not expecting to see a short, muddy, blood-splattered boy on the streets and didn't know quite what to make of him, me. The soldier called Zeke brandished his musket menacingly at me. "Who are you?"

"Eli," I said, proud of my strong voice. "I live there." With a sweep of my arm I indicated our house. I don't think he believed me.

Zeke cast a wary look about. "There were two of you. Where's the other one?"

"My brother's in the azaleas," I said.

"What's he doing there?" John asked.

"Are you Yankee spies?" Zeke asked.

"Spies!" I shook my head, amazed they'd come up with such an absurd notion. "Do I sound like a spy, sir?" I tapped my head. "This is a Rebel cap."

"You can't be too careful these days," Zeke said, not admitting the possibility he was wrong. "If you're Confederate, why did you hide from us?"

I was eyeing John, whose eyes were fixed on the hedge, somewhat skeptically. He pushed aside a twig of leaves. "I see...."

I coolly shuffled my way between him and the azaleas and commenced to tell my story, making sure I had both his and Zeke's attention. "We weren't hiding. We're about procuring medicine for our sick... sister, but we lost our money in the hedge." I paused. Oh, yes, I had their attention. I continued, "My brother is searching for it, but if we don't find it soon, she most likely will die."

Zeke took a huge step back. "What's wrong with your sister? Where is she now?"

"At the cave. She has a fever and chills and this rash and blisters all over her face." I left the rest to their imaginations.

"Smallpox!" John threw his hands in front of his face, as though he might catch this dreadful disease simply from looking at me. He and Zeke couldn't move away fast enough.

"The hospital's down the road," John called over his shoulder, hastening in the opposite direction so fast he almost tripped over his own feet.

I regretted scaring the soldiers. They were probably nice fellows. But I had to consider the consequences of my actions, the way Mama said. Should I turn the Yankee over to them, I didn't think they would treat him kindly.

"Thank you," the Yankee said as soon as the soldiers were out of sight.

He wasn't supposed to be a gentleman. He was supposed to be a... an ungentleman, I concluded, for want of a better word. "Stop saying that!"

Within minutes after we collapsed on the steps of my house, the front door burst open and Nat rushed out. "Nat!" I was delighted and bewildered to see him. "Why aren't you at the cave with Mama?"

He looked me up and down, eyebrow lifted almost to his hairline. "I read your note, Lizzie."

"Oh! Is Mama upset?" I asked, knowing full well that she was.

"She sent Uncle Morris for Father. Father told her not to fret. He'll find you. I came for Father's pistol. Does that answer your question?"

Before I could answer, he trailed a finger down my face. "You're dirty and bloody, Lizzie, and wearing my clothes. And you're with him." He tipped his head at the Yankee, who had fainted. "Which army did you join? Confederate? Or Yankee?"

Again, guilt nipped at my neck, but what was done was done. I couldn't go back and undo it. "I'm in no mood for your sarcasm, Nat. Help me get the soldier inside."

Nat planted his feet firmly on the porch. "He's a Yankee."

I was hot, thirsty, and rapidly losing patience. The knowledge that Papa was scouring the countryside for me did little to improve my humor. "A wounded Yankee," I shot back.

With a scowl of disapproval, Nat thrust his arms around the soldier's chest and lifted him to his feet. They tottered for a moment, and I thought they'd both tumble down the steps. But Nat was strong for his age and regained control. "Where do you want him?" he asked with a low growl.

"My room," I replied just as testily.

His eyebrow rose higher.

How I despised having to depend on Nat. He was my younger brother, but lately he treated me as though *I* were the baby in the family. I was too happy to see him to quarrel, though, so I said, "It's just for now, Nat. We'll remove him to the hospital as soon as I've attended his wounds and rested." I climbed the stairs.

When I folded back the quilt on my canopied bed, Nat regarded me, stone silent. I could imagine the thoughts tumbling around in his head. They were in mine, too. I felt like a traitor, giving refuge to the enemy. Because of the Yankees, my lovely city lay devastated. Many of the homes, where friends and neighbors had lived and laughed and loved, now stood empty, nothing left but sad reminders of happier times.

Nat dumped the Yankee on my bed, none too gently.

"Water," the Yankee whispered.

Seeing him a breath away from death brought back a rush of memories I was trying desperately to forget: the bodies in the field, the nameless soldiers, Private Arnold. Gray fog surrounded me, suffocated me. I reached out to the bedpost, lest I fall. My hand slid down.

I awoke in the armchair, Nat waving a fan at my face, his eyes big and fearful. He slipped an arm around my waist. "You're sick, Lizzie. I'm taking you to Mother."

I whisked his hand away. "I'm not sick, Nat. I'm...."

How could I describe the incredible horror of bloodshed and war and death? I couldn't. I prayed that Nat should never witness anything so cruel.

The Yankee was thrashing about, muttering, "Thirsty... Mother... Father...."

The soldier's words again reminded me of Willie and Joseph. He, too, had a mother, a father, somewhere, who were waiting for word from their son. I had to save him, for them. I took a couple of deep breaths to gather my wits then went over to the bed and rested a hand on the wounded man's brow. "He's burning up, Nat. Fetch me water, bandages, lint, alcohol, iodine, whatever Papa has to clean wounds."

"I shan't leave you alone with him."

"Go, Nat. He can't harm me. Look at him. He's helpless as a baby."

Nat grumbled all the way out the door and down the hallway, and I proceeded to remove the soldier's tattered remnants of shirt. The bandage was soaked clean through and smelled like rotten logs in the woods. My nose wrinkled, but I was getting used to the odor of death. What terrible times we live in to admit to such a thing.

I held the cup of water Nat brought to the Yankee's lips. He drank greedily. After his thirst was quenched, I cleaned and dressed his wound then bathed his face. Once the dirt and blood were removed, I discovered he was younger than I had thought—seventeen perhaps, Willie's age, eighteen at the most.

All this time Nat stood at the foot of the bed, his face a sickly shade of gray. Although Joseph planned to become a surgeon, like Papa, the sight of blood made Nat and Willie ill. Nat left once, returned with a shirt, and pulled it on the Yankee. He believed it was not proper for me to see a man's bare chest, unaware I had witnessed worse.

"Why are you blue, Lizzie?" he asked.

Nat was too observant. I could not tell my little brother the cruelties I had seen on the battlefield, on our land where small animals once lived, and birds built their nests, and children played, but that now was hardly more than a graveyard. I smoothed the covers around the Yankee, who was sleeping restlessly, and decided to tell Nat enough to satisfy him, no more.

"Come downstairs," I said. "I'll make tea."

Chapter 10

"How can I make tea when there is no tea? It's so unfair, Nat! So unfair!"

I slumped into a kitchen chair and buried my face in my hands. My spirits sank lower than the Mississippi River. Feeling extremely sorry for myself, I counted all the things unfair in my life. "My room has holes in the wall. A Yankee lies on my white sheets, getting them grimy with sweat and blood and who knows what. Papa cares for the sick soldiers more than he cares for me. And I have no tea!"

Nat swiveled my chair around and knelt before me. "The tea isn't what troubles you, Lizzie." He took the cap, which was now a splattered black and brown, off my head. "This is. Where did you get it?"

My resolution to spare Nat the harsh realities of battle forsook me, and I poured out the whole story, from the moment I left the cave, to finding the Yankee, to the present. Nat listened, his face unreadable. When I faltered he waited, never rushing me. After I finished, he was silent.

He never called me a coward, a traitor, or a shame to the family, all the things I was calling myself. Instead he said, "Don't do that again, Lizzie."

"You don't have to tell me."

He patted my hand. "It's settled then," he said. "What about the Yankee?"

"As soon as my weary bones have recovered I'll take him to the hospital."

"From the looks of him he won't survive that long."

I rubbed my arms against a sudden chill. "I shan't think of that, Nat. No one should die alone, away from family, friends."

"He's a Yankee."

"I don't wish to discuss him with you, Nat. My throat is dry. It hurts to talk. Do we have milk?"

"No, the neighbor's cow disappeared."

Her misfortune was expected. "Poor animal. Poor us. Soon we'll be eating mulberry leaves, same as the horses and mules."

Nat got to his feet. "You shall have your tea, Lizzie."

And he was off on one of his mysterious missions, to where I hadn't a notion and cared still less. Tired beyond belief, I kneaded the back of my neck with my fingers, the way Aunt Lois does bread dough. I tipped my head forward then back. My neck popped like bacon frying in the skillet. I sniffed. What was that disgusting odor? I lifted the front of Nat's shirt, turned up my nose. It was me.

According to Mama, I wasn't exactly a lady, but I preferred to smell like one. What I wouldn't give for a warm bath. Luxuries such as bathing were almost unheard of now, however, so I went back to my room and had to satisfy myself with a fresh dress, a clean face, and a comb to my hair.

"Your tea is served, Miss Elizabeth," Nat said, coming into my room and giving me a sweeping bow.

"Tea!" I fell into the chair, giggling at the comical sight of Nat, a china cup with a ribbon of steam swirling above it perched daintily in his fingers. Only he could come up with tea when there was none. "Where did you find it?"

He grinned, delighted he had pleased me. "There's a sassafras tree close by the cave. The roots, boiled, make fairly good tea, if you like the stuff."

I was indeed fortunate to have such an extraordinary brother. I sipped slowly. The tea trickled down my throat, warming me all the way to my toes. "It's delicious," I said. Of course, after my recent experience in the rifle pits with water from a canteen that quite possibly had come from the river, sour milk would taste like heaven.

Nat held out a hand. "Mother needs to know you're all right, Lizzie."

Hand in hand, we descended the spiral staircase and met Mama and Papa, climbing up.

Mama wrapped her arms around me. A tear rolled down her cheek. "Elizabeth, honey. You're safe."

She sprinkled kisses over my face. "I was so afraid … not knowing where you were. How you were. If I'd ever see you again."

Papa was a different matter. His face was darker than thunder. Tight lines formed around his mouth. His voice boomed, not one bit of gentleness in it. "You disappoint me, Elizabeth Susan Stamford, to be so selfish as to think only of yourself. Your note distressed your mother, and me. We imagined…."

He cleared his throat. His jaw danced. "War is not a game, Elizabeth. The army is no place for a girl. There are bad men…." Deep breath. "At least you came to your senses before it was too late."

I flinched under his harsh words. The only time Papa used my three names was when he was very angry with me. I couldn't fault him. I was a wretched, unworthy, wicked daughter and deserved his reprimand. I regretted the fact that I had brought disgrace to myself and to my family, but I refused to be ashamed of what I had done, except that I had failed.

"I followed my heart, Papa," I said, "the way Mama told me. I made a mistake. Haven't you ever?"

Mama's and Papa's eyes met. Then Papa laid a big hand on the side of my face. "I've made my share of mistakes, Elizabeth. I'm sure your mother has also. Hopefully we've learned a lesson from each of them. I ought to punish you for the worry you caused your mother by your thoughtless conduct."

Whatever his punishment was, nothing could be worse than the past two days.

"You ought to," I said in agreement.

The lines about his mouth softened. "I believe you've suffered more than enough, Elizabeth. I believe you've witnessed things no young lady should ever behold. That is punishment enough." He held me close. He was trembling.

He forgave me. Perhaps someday I'd forgive myself. In the meantime, there was the matter of the wounded soldier upstairs. Sometimes I wished I were more like Nat and thought before I spoke. Unfortunately, I usually jumped right in, rather than preparing Mama and Papa gently for my announcements. And that's what I did now.

"Papa. I have a Yankee in my room."

Mama's face went from red, to pink, to gray, to Magnolia blossom white. She fluttered her fan. "A Federal soldier in my home, Elizabeth? In your room? I declare!"

Papa's brown eyes bore into mine. "Perhaps you'd care to explain, Elizabeth."

The bloody scene on the battlefield flashed before me: the men, the corpses, silent forever, the Yankee, clinging to life. To tell about it was to relive the nightmare. "I can't, Papa."

Sweet brother Nat came to my rescue. By the time we reached my room, Mama was shaking her head and Papa was scowling, until he saw the wounded soldier. Then he went to work.

৪০০৪

Later, Papa spread the sheet over the Yankee, who had lapsed into sleep, or unconsciousness. Papa washed his hands and rolled down his shirtsleeves. "The soldier has an infection, Elizabeth, but he's young and strong. God willing, he'll survive. Nothing more I can do for him now. Time will heal him or…"

He didn't have to finish.

Papa studied me. "How did you know what to do?"

I shrugged. "I've watched you. I wasn't sure how to stop the fever, though, except for keeping him cool with wet rags." I smiled a little. "Did I do all right?"

He returned my smile. "I could not have done better myself, Elizabeth. Most young ladies would faint at such a sight."

"I'm not most young ladies. I did have some queasy moments, though," I added.

Papa chuckled. "I appreciate your spirit, Elizabeth, even though you try my patience at times."

"Then you have no objections that I brought the Yankee here?"

A thin cloud flitted across Papa's face. "Objections? I have several. First, you put yourself in great danger, Elizabeth. He might have shot you. Did you never consider that possibility?"

A gasp escaped from Mama. Papa patted her arm, the way Nat had mine, all the while watching me.

"I thought of it," I said. "I also thought about shooting him, but he reminded me of Willie and Joseph, and I couldn't. You'd have done the same."

Papa pushed out his mouth and stroked his whiskers, the way he did when deep in thought. He cast a sidelong glance at the Yankee. "You have a point, Elizabeth, which brings us to my second concern. He is a Federal soldier and, as such, now our prisoner."

I had never thought about what would happen to the Yankee afterward. "You will send him to prison then?" I asked.

Papa skimmed a look from me to Nat, lingering on my brother.

"We attend to the wounded, both Confederate and Federal, in our hospital. Should the soldier survive, he will spend the rest of this war in a Confederate prison camp. I cannot release him to return to his regiment and the battlefield to kill our boys, or to be killed himself."

Papa let out a long breath. "At least in prison he'll live and one day go home to his family. Many others will not."

I wondered if that was true. Joseph had written a letter once about the number of soldiers who died of disease, starvation, and filthy conditions in the prison camps. But those were Yankee prisons. Ours were different, were they not? I couldn't shake the dismal feeling that all prisons were much the same.

Papa turned to Mama. "I have a request, Susan. Every cot at the hospital is occupied. We have so many wounded that some men even sleep on blankets on the floor. The tents we set up on the hospital grounds have no room, either. Another hospital or home might have space for the boy, but he's in no condition to be moved anytime soon. Susan, since this is your home as much as mine, I'm asking your permission to let the young soldier stay here?"

"Here!" Mama exclaimed. "You can't mean that!"

"But I do."

Mama had to sit down. She was too distressed to even flick her fan, but she seldom opposed Papa's wishes. "Do what you think best, Charles."

Papa kissed her lightly on the cheek. "Thank you, Susan. Morris shall see to the soldier's needs in my absence. I'll leave medicine, bandages. When he's able to eat, Lois can prepare his food. I'll look in on him whenever possible."

Mama managed a half-hearted smile. "Will you find time for a visit to the cave, when you're out and about?"

Papa gathered her up in his strong arms. "Most definitely. In fact, the hospital can spare me a few hours tonight. I'll take supper with you and the children."

She snuggled in Papa's arms. "I'm afraid we have only the usual."

Nat pulled two apples from his pocket and handed them to Mama. "You could make a brown Betty, Mother."

First sassafras tea and now ripe, red apples. I wondered what else he concealed in those magical pockets.

Papa said, "What a splendid idea."

"We'll dine at the cave, by candlelight," Mama said, getting caught up in Papa's enthusiasm.

"Like old times," Papa said, carrying her down the stairs.

"The soldier's mother must be worried sick," Mama said, her gentle soul concerned for some woman far, far away. "You should write her a letter, Elizabeth. Tell her that her son is safe."

She was thinking of Willie and Joseph, as were Papa and Nat, and I, and how many weeks had passed since we'd heard from them. "I'll ask the soldier his name and where his home is," I said.

Papa stopped so abruptly that I had to dodge aside to keep from colliding with him. He set Mama down. "By heaven, Elizabeth!"

he said. "You'll do nothing of the kind! I am much troubled by the number of shells falling in the city. The house is in great danger. I shall allow you nowhere near it. Had I foreseen what was to come, I'd have insisted you and your mother and brother leave Vicksburg months ago. The best I can do now is see you all to the cave."

"The cave is perfect, Papa," I said, and meant it.

Chapter 11

A̲FTER SUPPER AND MAMA'S brown Betty, which there was hardly enough of for a family of four and two servants, I strummed my guitar. Mama, Papa, and Nat sang and clapped hands. Nat's voice even sounded halfway pleasant tonight. Aunt Lois and Uncle Morris swayed to the music, like willow trees in a gentle spring breeze. That we could sing and enjoy ourselves amid the shelling and destruction of our fair city might seem strange. But why should we not? Save for Joseph and Willie our family was together, giving us a brief reprieve from the bitter taste of hatred and war, from the uncertainty of our everyday existence.

The Moseleys from a neighboring cave, attracted by our lively airs, came by with their three little ones. Since our cave was too small for so many, we spilled outside, but stayed close enough to dart into the cave should the mortars threaten. The Moseley girl, Anna, who was four, perched herself in my lap and picked at the guitar strings with her short, stubby fingers. The boys, George and Raymond, ages three and six, spotted Nat's woodcarvings. Before he could protect his precious works of art, they each snatched up a handful and raced around the trees and shrubs, laughing with mischievous delight.

Nat sprinted after them yelling, "If you break anything, I'll turn you into frogs."

Nobody believed him for a minute.

The boys squealed louder and taunted him unmercifully. "You got to catch us first."

There weren't many places two small boys could hide. They made the mistake of rushing inside the cave, where Nat trapped them behind Mama's rocking chair. He advanced, putting on his best mean face, which made the boys giggle all the more. They finally skittered down on the ground and began to play with the flying machine and sailboat, Nat in the midst of them, explaining in great detail how they worked. The boys concentrated on his every word, never blinking an eye.

With children around, the world seemed a brighter place. The peril from the battlefield didn't enter their heads. They played their games as before and thought living under the earth quite an adventure. Oh, that I could. I was trying.

Being little boys, they soon grew tired of sitting still, bounced up, and said, "Play more music, Lizbeth."

I thrummed the guitar until my fingers protested. Anna danced with Nat. All too soon a shell exploded directly overhead, ending our glorious evening and sending us running for cover. The Moseleys and their children scuttled to their cave, one of Nat's carved figures gripped tightly in each of the boys' grubby fists, his compliments.

"Why did you give them your carvings?" I asked as we huddled in the cave.

"They fancied them."

Life was that simple for Nat. When Papa departed for the hospital later, Mama settled into her rocking chair with her knitting. Uncle Morris went to the house to attend to the wounded Yankee. Since I had lost the letter I had started to Willie in the entrenchments, I searched the cave for pen and paper to begin a new one. I found not a scrap, nor anything to write with. Unbidden tears floated dreadfully close to the surface of my eyes. I had paper in my desk at home. I'd just have to get it, regardless of Papa's orders. Might I discover some hidden courage there, as well?

𝝔𝒪𝒢

Early Sunday morning Uncle Morris returned. His report on the Yankee was not good. "I've seen soldier boys what look just like him afore they leave this world. He ain't gonna live to welcome the sunset."

Mama tied her bonnet. "We'll say a special prayer for him, Morris, and for his family. After church you can fetch a note to Dr.

Stamford about the young man's condition. Perhaps he can perform a miracle. He has, you know."

"Yes'm, Mistress. I seen 'em with my own eyes."

Mama threw on her shawl, slipped her hands into her gloves, and turned to me. "We'll be home soon, honey. See that you rest. Take care of your sister, Nathan."

She kissed my brow. Then she, Uncle Morris, and Aunt Lois went out.

I must look pretty wretched for Mama to allow me to miss church.

Nat reached into his pocket and withdrew a handful of apricots. "I thought you'd like these for breakfast, Lizzie."

"Where on earth did you find apricots?"

"On an apricot tree."

"Of course, how silly of me." I took a bite. The apricot was delicious. I held one out to Nat.

"I already had some."

"Did not."

At my coaxing, he ate half of them.

When we had finished the last plump apricot, I arose and started outside.

"What are you doing?" Nat asked.

Lately, that had become one of his favorite questions. "Not that it's any of your business, but I'm about fetching my paper and pen from the house. How else can I write Willie and Joseph? And the soldier's Mama?"

"Mother says you're to rest."

"I am rested. Move out of my way."

"Stubborn," he said.

"You ought to know."

He escorted me.

Chapter 12

SUNLIGHT STREAMED THROUGH the windows of my room, pooling around the Yankee's face in an unsettling glow. His hair, dark as night, clung in matted clumps to his moist brow. Sweat stained his pillow. His chest made no movement. Like Private Arnold. Like the soldiers in the field.

The room started to spin. Birds chirped in my ears. An odd noise, like an animal in pain, rumbled in my throat. I braced my hands on the mattress to hold myself up. The Yankee had died, the way Uncle Morris predicted. Alone. Nobody to comfort him, to murmur soothing words, to say a prayer. His mother and father would never again see his smile, hear his voice, or feel his touch.

A battle of conflicting emotions raged within me. He was a Yankee, some fellow I had stumbled upon, quite by accident. Not my concern. I didn't even know his name. Didn't wish to know his name. Nevertheless, he had been polite, a true gentleman, I think. Now his pulse no longer beat. The war would go on. Everybody would forget he even existed. Except for his mother and father. And me.

I pulled my shawl tightly around my shoulders. "Nat, he's... he's..."

A faint flicker of eyelid. A slight quiver of finger.

And I let out a shriek that surely sank the entire Federal fleet.

Nat caught me as I bolted for the door. "Don't panic, Lizzie. The Yankee's...."

"Panic! A dead man has come back to life, before my very eyes, and you tell me not to panic." I babbled like a crazy person, but couldn't help it.

Nat shook me. "Calm yourself, Lizzie. The Yankee is alive. Always has been. The dead do not sweat."

Sweat? Oh! I jerked my head to look at the pillow. I ought to have noticed. I did, I recalled vaguely, but did not think it important. I nodded in amazement at this brother I hardly recognized anymore. The first time he had beheld the Yankee's wounds, he almost fainted. Now he was coolly surveying the Yankee, who had lifted himself up and was leaning on his good elbow. His eyes were on Nat. "Eli?" he asked softly.

Nat's jaw danced in clear annoyance. With me, I imagine, for starting this whole Eli pretense. "I'm Nathan," he said.

The Yankee cast a quizzical glance at me. "You can't be... Eli was... man."

I smoothed the wrinkles in my skirt. No wonder the poor fellow was bewildered. Today I bore little resemblance to the Eli he had known. Eli had existed only briefly, but in his short life he learned many unforgettable lessons. Though my disguise had worked, I had no plans to continue the deception. How could I explain about Eli to the Yankee, without adding another lie to my already numerous ones? Tell the truth, Mama would say. So I did, at least the way I saw it.

"I'm Elizabeth, Eli's sister." I inclined my head at Nat. "Nathan is our brother. Mm, Eli is no longer with us."

Nat scowled. "Let's go, Lizzie."

"In a minute. May I get you anything, soldier? Food? Water?"

"Thank you, no." The Yankee looked me over warily. "I recall Eli was... a Rebel."

"We are Confederate," I said. "This is our home. You were wounded, but the hospital was too far distant, so Eli brought you here."

The Yankee sighed and eased back on the pillow. "Tell Eli... he has... beautiful sister."

Beautiful? Me? I never fancied anyone calling me beautiful. Oh, Papa said I was his pretty little honey sometimes. But Papas say things like that. I was obliged to admit the poor fellow's fever had returned, and he was delirious. Or else he had bad eyesight.

"Thank Eli... for saving... my life," the Yankee added.

Land sakes! He was the politest Yankee I had ever met. The only Yankee, actually. He was not at all what I expected a Yankee to be.

"I'll tell him," I said. Why admit that I was Eli when I would never see this soldier after the war?

"Lizzie! Get your writing paper and let's go."

Nat's patience had reached an end. Since I was anxious to not cause Mama more distress, and Papa would arrive soon to attend to the soldier, I retrieved my last two sheets of paper, as well as envelopes, from my desk. "I'm ready, Nat."

"It's about time."

"Miss Elizabeth."

I tossed a look at the Yankee. "Yes?"

"Would you mind to… leave me something to… write on?"

"You wish to write?"

A wistful expression passed over the Yankee's face. "Haven't… seen my mother and father for months."

His request touched me deeply. We had not seen my brothers for months, either, but at least we had heard from them and knew they were well, at last account. The Yankee's mother would welcome news from her son, but he was too weak to sit up, much less hold pen in hand. The least I could do was write it for him. Mama wouldn't object. In fact, she had suggested I do so yesterday. I ignored the fact Papa had bade me stay in the cave. I'd worry about that later.

"Save your strength, soldier," I said. "I'll write your letter."

His lip curved up in what I suppose was intended for a smile, though it more resembled a grimace. His arm must be quite painful. "Why did you… your brother… rescue me?" he asked.

"She shouldn't have," Nat said getting testier by the minute. He used to never sass me, but this war had changed everything, including Nat.

"She?"

I glared bolts of lightning at Nat. He clamped his mouth shut, but his jaw continued to dance, in that Stamford family trait. "This won't take long, Nat," I said.

"Then hurry. I shan't tell another untruth for you, Lizzie."

He preferred the word untruth to lie. I saw no difference. "I never asked you to."

He pulled a chair beside the bed for me to sit on, and I commenced to pen a letter to the Yankee's family. "What are you called, soldier?"

"Ben."

"Just Ben?"

"Private Benjamin Clayton, 76th Ohio Infantry."

His voice was somewhat stronger now, and the color was returning to his face.

"You're a long way from home, soldier."

"Home." He let out a slow breath. "How I wish I were there."

I could hear Willie and Joseph yearning for the same thing. "The war won't last forever, soldier. Then you'll go home." Alive, I added silently, thanks to Papa.

The Yankee looked at me doubtfully. His eyes were the blue of a robin's egg and quite nice, though sorrowful.

"Are all Southern women as kind and gentle as you?" he asked.

More compliments. Feeling the heat rise from my neck to my cheeks, I couldn't think of one sensible word to say, so I lowered my eyes. Mama would be proud.

Nat had plenty to say, however. "Yankee, you are staring at my sister."

I peered at the Yankee through my lashes. He looked properly reproved.

"I don't mean to offend your sister, Nathan," he said, "or you. It's just… I had this picture in my mind of Southerners, but you're no different than me, except for that slow drawl you have when you speak."

Flustered by the Yankee's boldness and by Nat's conduct, I bent over the letter and scribbled furiously:

> Dear Mr. Clayton and Mrs. Clayton,
>   I am dropping you a few lines in regard to your son,

Private Benjamin Clayton. Do not be alarmed. He is
alive and well, but suffers from a wound to the arm.
He sends his love and is very anxious to see you.

Before I could write another line, the war intruded. Shells—I
swear there were hundreds of them—howled outside the windows.
I jumped nearly out of my skin. Ink spilled, a blob on white paper.
With one swift motion, Nat shoved me to the floor, where we
crouched beside the bed, listening and praying. The house whined
and creaked, as one ball after another thudded to earth or exploded
in midair. Nat clung to me, this half-child, half-man, who one minute was my protector, the next in need of protection.

"Does this happen often?" the Yankee asked. His voice crackled
more with anger than fear, I think.

"Day. Night." Nat said. "But you know. You're one of them."

I did not like speaking with someone I could not see, so I rose to
my feet. The Yankee's eyes, sunken bruises in his face, held a look of
pity, as well as fury. "I never realized," he said. "'Tisn't... right."

"Nothing's right these days," I said, "since you Yankees came to
Vicksburg."

A shell struck the gallery outside my bedroom, sending a frag-
ment of shrapnel through the glassless window that landed not
three feet from us. Nat sprang up, grabbed my hand, and propelled
me toward the door. "We've got to get back to the cave, Lizzie."

"But the Yankee! We can't leave him."

"I'm to watch over you," Nat said, his face a mask of grim determination, "not him."

Another blast quieted my protest, and I went willingly. At the
end of the hallway, I heard voices, drifting up from the floor below.
Thinking it was Papa and Uncle Morris, I galloped down the stairs,
ignoring Nat's frantic "Lizzie, come back!"

I flew into the parlor. Slid to a halt. Cried, "Oh!" as a giant of a
man slammed his rifle against Mama's tall mirror that hung between
the windows.

Chapter 13

G LASS TINKLED, SHATTERED, sailed in all directions.
"Oh!" I cried again.

And the giant turned, his eyes glittering with fire that quickly changed to curiosity. He thrust his cap back on his head and roared at me. "Well now, missy, who might you be?"

My mind went completely empty. I had not the slightest idea who I was. I saw only the giant's face, with its scraggly gray whiskers. Greasy, black hair dripped from under his cap. Out of the corner of my eye I glimpsed a second man, his nose quite large and crooked. Books from the shelves lay around his feet, pages torn out, shredded remnants.

The giant moved closer. "Are ya deaf, missy? Speak up."

He stood so near I could smell his foul breath. I crossed my arms and willed my limbs to not buckle under me. Confused thoughts raced through my head. Who were these men? Why were they destroying our property? They were clad in blue so they must be Yankees. Why were they not with their regiment? Unless.... They were deserters. They had to be.

The soldier with the crooked nose circled to my right and laid a hand on my shoulder. My skin crawled at his touch.

"You are a pretty little thing," he said.

My heart thumped against my ribs. My head pounded. What would they do to me? To Nat? Nat... I had to warn him, lest he come looking for me. Fearing for my brother's life, I shrugged off Crooked Nose's hand, spun around, and bumped into a third soldier, entering the room. His hair was the reddest red I had ever seen. A smattering of freckles, the same color as his hair, dotted his nose and cheekbones. A bulging apron, Aunt Lois's, something clanking inside it, dangled from his hand.

He blinked. "Ma'am?" He appeared quite uncomfortable. "Excuse me, miss." Bowing, he stepped aside for me to pass.

Not waiting to question my unexpected good luck, I darted past the Yankee, before he changed his mind, and had reached the hallway, when a voice behind me yelled, "Hey! Stupid! She's gettin' away. Stop her!"

"Hold on, miss," Red Hair said almost apologetically. He snagged my arm and ushered me back into the parlor. "Don't try to escape," he whispered in my ear. "I shan't hurt you."

I desired not to test his words. I twisted and turned, stomped on his toes and kicked his leg in an attempt to wriggle free. It did me not one ounce of good. Red Hair held me quite easily, without so much as a whimper, and asked, "When did we start fighting with women and children, Mack?"

Mack, the giant, spat a stream of brown liquid on Mama's wooden floor. "Ain't fightin' nobody, Red. Just want some information from the girl."

The Yankee fancied information, did he? My blood boiled. How dare he... they... smash our mirror, destroy Papa's library, and then expect.... Yankees be hanged. My impulsive self took over. "You'll get nothing from me, you... you impertinent Yankee scoundrels. You're nothing but thieves and... and ruffians and deserters and a disgrace to the uniform you wear. I ought to thank you, though. Because of sniveling, weak-minded renegades like yourselves, our Confederate army will whip you and leave you wishing you'd never set eyes on Vicksburg."

"Miss, hush," Red said in warning.

He needn't have bothered. These fellows had no conscience. My words flew over their heads like dandelion fluff.

Mack let out a horselaugh. Half his teeth were missing. "You're a little spitfire, ain't you, missy. I like spunky gals."

"She shore is an unfriendly lass," Crooked Nose said.

"Aw, let her alone, Mack, Luke," Red said. "I got the silver and some china, what wasn't broken. There's nothing else here, not even food. We might as well skedaddle, before the girl's folks come looking for her."

Mack growled. "A big fancy house like this has to have money, jewelry, something of value."

"Confederate money ain't worth spit," Luke said, "but a bottle of whiskey'd taste mighty good about now."

"Quit thinking about your stomach. I'm bettin' the little gal here will lead us to more valuables, like this." Mack reached out and yanked my locket off my neck, breaking the chain as he did. "Where's the rest of your jewelry, missy? And your ma's?"

I was somewhere between scared senseless and furious, but my anger overcame my terror. This Yankee scoundrel had stolen my precious locket. I wasn't about to let him have it, not without a fight. I grabbed at the chain. "That's mine! Give it to me!"

Laughing, Mack fended off my flailing hands and jammed the locket in his pocket. "Now, missy, let's see what's upstairs."

"Nothing's there," I said, too quickly.

Save for Nat and Private Clayton.

"I don't believe you." Mack shoved me toward the stairs.

I couldn't let the Yankees find Nat. I gulped and said the first thing that entered my head. "My papa will be here any second. My brothers. Unless you fancy facing all ten of them, you'd better get out of here."

"Ten, huh?" Mack chewed, spat, guffawed, and gave me another push. "Odds sound about right. What do you say, boys?"

Luke grinned. Red frowned. They continued up the stairs.

With each step we took that led us closer to the second floor, I said a silent prayer that Nat had climbed out a window and had gone to fetch Papa. We were halfway up the stairs when a floorboard above us creaked. Nat had not heard my prayer. All eyes turned upward. I heard three clicks as rifle hammers were cocked.

Mack leaned into my face. "Who's up there, missy? How many? Are they armed?"

"What if she really does have ten brothers?" Red asked, sounding anxious. "We can't tackle that many."

"She don't," Luke said.

For what seemed like an eternity Mack towered over me. Mean-
er eyes in a man I had never beheld. Dizzy thoughts swam in my
head. My ears roared. Nat evidently was still in my room. What on
earth was he doing? Could he not be quieter? "Nobody's there," I
said. "I told you."

"You're a liar, missy." Mack nodded at Luke. "Shoot anything that
moves," he said.

"With pleasure." Luke crept up the stairs.

"Fetch the girl along, Red, in case some Reb brother or friend of
hers is waitin' to ambush us."

"And let her warn whoever's up there we're coming?" Red said.
"I've got a better idea. I'll tie her up and leave her here. Keep her
outta our hair that way."

"Do it then." Another thud distracted Mack. "There's more'n one,
for sure. We'll sneak up on 'em. Catch 'em by surprise. Tie the girl
good, Red, stuff somethin' in her mouth, and you watch our backs.
More Rebs might be outside."

Mack and Luke vanished around the curve of the staircase, and
Red commenced to tie my hands behind my back. He ordered me
to sit and then followed the others.

Luckily, Red was not very good at tying knots. I had wriggled my
hands free by the time he was out of sight. I scrambled after him,
crouched on the top step, and peeked down the hallway. Empty.
Voices floated through the open door of Papa and Mama's room.
Across the hall, the door to my room was shut. If I was very quiet,
I could make it to my room, without alerting the Yankees. I tiptoed
to the door, silently pushed it open, ducked inside and into Nat's
arms. "Nat," I whispered. "We have to get away before they find us.
Hurry. We'll climb to the ground from the gallery. Hurry."

Holding me with one arm, Nat shut the door with his other. He
propped a chair against it. Then he rested his hands on my shoulders. "You're babbling, Lizzie."

"But Nat, the Yankees…."

"Listen to me…."

"They're deserters, Nat. They're in Papa's room." My voice rose. "They'll come in here next."

Nat withdrew a revolver from his belt. "I know about the Yanks, Lizzie."

"You made the noises on purpose?"

"I hoped they'd bring you upstairs to investigate. Now get behind the chest. I'll take care of the Yanks."

My mouth was as dry as cotton in the fields. "Where did you get Papa's revolver?"

"His room."

"Is it loaded? Do you know how to shoot it?"

Nat shrugged. "The Yankee told me how to load it. Then I pull back the hammer. Aim. Squeeze the trigger."

The soldiers' voices carried clearly from the hallway, coming our way.

"And live with the knowledge you seriously wounded or perhaps killed a man?" I asked.

Doubt clouded Nat's eyes. "If I have to," he said thinly.

To take a life would destroy sensitive Nat. I bit my lip and silently counted to three, hoping to give myself courage. It did not. I was scared silly, but I took the Colt revolver out of Nat's hand. "Private Arnold taught me how to use a rifle."

Admitting to Nat I had never fired a shot served no purpose. Rifle or pistol, they worked the same. At least I told myself that. Holding the Colt in both my hands, my finger hooked in the trigger, I slowly faced the door. Nat stood helplessly at my side, torn between watching out for me and giving in to his fears. Nat isn't a coward. He just wants his life back. We all do.

Someone jiggled the doorknob. The chair rattled, but held. Perspiration trickled down my face and pooled in the hollow of my neck. The Colt weighed heavy in my hands. Then something crashed against the door, splintering it. The chair scooted across the floor. And Mack charged into the room.

Chapter 14

"HALT RIGHT THERE."
I know not where my courageous words came from, or what I should have done had Mack kept coming, but miracle of miracles, he skidded to a stop. I leveled the Colt at a spot between his eyes. We glared at each other, neither of us sure what to expect from the other.

Luke and Red crowded in behind him, but Mack held up a hand. They, too, froze. He must think me capable of firing the gun, or else he'd not be so cautious. I hoped he was right. I gripped the revolver tightly. Surely I couldn't miss at this close range.

Mack's shifty eyes darted from me to Nat and back. Then he tipped back his cap, grinned and said, "Well now, missy. Watcha' gonna do with that there pistol? Shoot me?"

He was challenging me. Church bells peeled in my ears. My head was as light as a spiderweb, but I dared not admit my fear. "You have exactly two minutes to get out of my house, Yankee, unless you fancy finding out."

Luke hooted. "The little lady givin' you trouble?"

Mack aimed his rifle at me. "Not so I noticed," he said.

I was sick and tired of facing guns, Yankee or Confederate. I had run away before. This time, for Nat's sake, and mine, I would stand firm. My palms wet, I clicked back the hammer. "One minute, Yankee." My knees knocked together so loudly he surely must hear them.

Mack swept the angle of his rifle from me to Nat. "Give me the gun, missy, and the boy won't get hurt."

Should I give him the revolver, we'd have no protection. I had to believe that Mack would not harm Nat, with the Colt staring him in the eyes. I decided to wait him out. For what seemed like hours I moved not a muscle. Neither did Mack. My fingers grew numb, and

I was wondering how long I could hold the gun and what would happen if I dropped it, when I heard the bed sheets rustle. A thud followed, as something—feet?—touched the floor.

"Let the boy and girl go," said a weak voice from behind me.

I glanced over my shoulder and beheld Private Clayton, his bad arm balanced in front of him, swaying on his feet. Then everything went crazy. An inhuman growl ripped through the air, and Nat shouted, "Lizzie, look out!" at the exact instant Mack struck my arm with a powerful blow that sent me reeling. The Colt leapt from my hands with a deafening explosion and skittered across the floor. I dived for it. Nat slid on his stomach. Mack scrambled. In the confusion, a bare foot shot out and kicked the revolver away. Somehow, I found it in my grasp. An ear-shattering boom bounded off the walls.

Silence engulfed the room. Mack staggered backward, his face contorted in a hideous, monstrous shape. His mouth moved, but no sound came out. A puddle of blood soaked through his shirt. Curse words spewed forth from his mouth. "She shot me! The little...."

With great haste, Red and Luke each hooked an arm around Mack and dragged him off, Mack sputtering and howling, "Let me at her. Let me...."

"Somebody might've heard that shot," Luke said, voice fading.

"Better not wait around to find out," Red said, barely audible.

Their footfalls grew silent.

But the echo of gunfire thundered in my ears. Over and over. Dark red rivers of blood stained Mama's floor. "I-I sh-shot him," I whimpered. "I d-didn't intend to. I didn't mean to. I...."

Nat eased the Colt from my fingers and cradled me in his arms.

Private Clayton lowered himself beside us. "That was a brave thing you did, Miss Elizabeth," he said. "You saved your brother's life, and mine."

Brave? A sound that started as a laugh but ended up a pitiful moan bubbled in my throat. Pictures of the dead soldiers in the field, their bodies covered with blood and dirt and flies, flooded before me. Private Arnold was brave. The soldiers were brave. I was not. I hid in the trenches. "What if he d-dies?" I asked, choking at the thought. "What about his f-family? They'll h-hate me."

"You defended yourself, Lizzie," Nat said gently. "I ought to have." With a finger he wiped away my tears. "Please, Lizzie, don't cry."

I sniffled. "I'm not."

"You are."

"So...."

A crystal-clear teardrop clung to Nat's eyelash. "So cry."

Through a misty curtain, I noted Private Clayton was watching us, somewhat anxiously. His face was as white as my lace curtains once were, before the shells and smoke from the fires turned them to gray. He looked about to faint. My sobs slowed to hiccups. I cast aside the past few minutes for more immediate concerns, and to save my sanity, and rose clumsily to my feet. "You should be in bed, Private Clayton," I said. "Come on with you now."

He refused my offered hand. "I can manage." He lumbered up and immediately tumbled down.

A crooked smile creased the corner of his mouth. "Perhaps you could give me a hand, Elizabeth." His brow puckered. "May I call you Elizabeth?"

"Uh-uh." Great granny's pantalets. What was it about this Yankee that left me unable to utter even a simple yes? He was a Yankee for heaven's sake, the meanest, the lowest of God's creatures. He was also wounded, weak, and a good-looking fellow. I know my ears turned pink, as I stammered some nonsense like "If you wish."

But Nat would not allow me to touch the Yankee. Without so much as a word, he thrust his shoulder under Private Clayton's arm, propelled him to the bed, and dropped him, quite roughly in my opinion, on the rumpled sheets.

Private Clayton was good-natured I must say. He told Nat, "Thank you," very politely. To me he said, "Elizabeth, my friends call me Ben."

Nat's jaw did that little dance. "We're not your friends."

Such hostility I had never witnessed in my brother. A fig on this war. Another reason I loathed it. Nat was struggling to be a man and, to my dismay, succeeding fairly well. My baby brother no longer existed save in age. Before me stood an intense young man, old beyond his years. I felt a hundred. I had possibly killed one Yankee, a scoundrel, true, but still a human being. Now another Yankee wanted to be my friend. I'd have to think about that.

Nat cupped my elbow in his hand. "I don't like the way you look, Lizzie. I'm taking you to Mother."

I flicked his hand away. "I can't face Mama. Not yet. Nat, I need a drink. Something strong. Fetch me Papa's brandy."

Talking to Nat was like talking to the wind. The words drifted away and were lost in the clouds, heard only by some distant folks, who knew not from whence they came.

"I'll make you tea," he said. He threw the private a look of distrust.

Private Clayton clearly read Nat's thoughts. "She's in no danger from me."

Nat gave a brief nod then left, trusting in a gentleman's word.

I clasped my hands, unclasped them, not knowing what to do with myself. The blast of the revolver drummed in my ears. Mack's look of disbelief and hatred haunted me, would haunt me forever. Whether he was enemy or friend I had no right to end his life. And the blood... Always the blood... Stains on the floor. I had to wash them, so Mama would not see. Something to keep me busy until Nat returned. I poured water from the washbowl on the spots, and scrubbed. And scrubbed. They wouldn't come off. I rubbed harder.

"Elizabeth."

The gentle Yankee voice brought me back to my senses. He was sitting up, observing me. He must think me a madwoman. Perhaps I was. Nat might dislike Private Clayton, but he wouldn't have left me alone with the Yankee had he not trusted him. I desperately wanted to talk, to make idle conversation, to get my mind off the deserters. I hesitated only a second before perching on the edge of my bed.

"Your brother is very fond of you, Elizabeth," Private Clayton said.

"Nat and I are close," I said.

I was thinking how easy he was to talk with, when out of the blue he asked, "Why did you pose as a man, Elizabeth?"

He caught me by surprise with that one. I blinked and studied Private Clayton, who had seen through my disguise. I was curious as to when and how he discovered my secret. Was it my hair? My voice? My walk? "You know? What gave me away?"

"Several things, actually. When you dressed my arm, Elizabeth, your hands were soft, not the hands of a man. And the way you held the revolver when you challenged Mack reminded me of how you had faced me, frightened, yet courageous, at least if I recall correctly, though my mind is a bit foggy. Your voice confirmed my suspicions." He offered me a weary smile. "I prefer you in skirts and petticoats, with your hair down and ribbons in it, like now."

Private Clayton was indeed bold. I twined my fingers around a loose thread of my skirt, my face hot. My mind searched for a polite response. The best I could do was blush furiously and stammer, "I borrowed Nat's clothes, for the army doesn't allow women, except to wash and cook and carry the soldiers' messages, but not to fight."

"With good reason, Elizabeth. War is too brutal for innocent young ladies like yourself." He looked me squarely in the eyes. "Why did you want to be a soldier?"

How could I explain? I shrugged. "I've asked myself that. At the time I believed that joining the army would make me a brave warrior. I would drive the Yankees away, save our city, and write my brothers about my great accomplishments."

"A noble goal."

"I know better now," I said

He smiled. "Perhaps you accomplished more than you realize."

"I doubt that."

"Believe it, Elizabeth. Take me for instance. I'm a Yankee, yet you brought me to your home."

"The hospital was too far."

"You nursed me."

"Papa attended to your injuries."

"You fed me."

"Uncle Morris fed you."

"Well, I do know you bathed me." Private Clayton's cheeks colored, as though he'd had too much sun. "You didn't have to care for me. Why did you?"

An idea occurred to me that must have been hiding in the back of my mind all along. "I wondered that myself, at first. I think I know now. My father is from New York, which makes him a Yankee."

Private Clayton's eyes twinkled. "Aha! That makes you a Yankee, too."

I corrected him pretty quick. "Only half. My mother was born in Mississippi."

"But your mother and father are together, Elizabeth. They see no difference. And I hear that General John Pemberton is from Pennsylvania, and his wife is a Virginian."

"That is true."

"If we were enemies, you would have left me to die. I certainly would have, save for you. It seems to me that, whether northern born or southern bred, we're all the same."

I found but one fault in what the Yankee was saying. "If we are the same, Ben, then why are you fighting with us?"

He considered that for several moments. I could tell he had doubts, the same as I. When he said, "We're here to free the slaves," it was more a question than a statement.

"The war isn't about our servants, Ben," I said, positive I was right. "Perhaps a little, but it's more about our way of life, I think. You Yankees are jealous of our fine homes and beautiful land, and you wish to take it for yourselves. You force us to live in caves, like animals, so we fight back. We're only defending what is ours. Would you not do the same, should we attack your home in Ohio?"

"I don't know anything about slaves, Elizabeth, save that it isn't right to own another person. And I most definitely would fight for my home."

Own? Yankees certainly had strange notions. "Aunt Lois and Uncle Morris are our family, Ben. This is their home. We love them. They love us. They want for nothing."

"Are they happy?"

"I suppose they are. I've never asked."

"I think I have much to learn," Ben said, brow wrinkled. "My friends and I enlisted to teach the Rebs a lesson. We also wanted to get away from our tedious lives. We'd never been anywhere, and the army was our chance to see places we'd never see otherwise. Four of us came south together. We thought our army would defeat the Rebs in a matter of two or three months. How wrong we were. My company has been in Vicksburg for weeks now; yet you Rebels do not surrender." His voice cracked. "Of my friends and me, only I am left."

I didn't care to hear about the Yankee and his friends or to think about more death, but the shells whizzed around us. I could not forget. My heart would ache forever for those whose hearts no longer beat. My mind filled with wails and shrieks and moans of agony. I bowed my head and started to tremble.

Then Ben did something unexpected. He put his good arm around me. "Are we friends, Elizabeth?" he asked.

"Friends? What on earth do you mean?"

"You called me Ben. Three times."

And Nat chose that moment to walk in.

Chapter 15

NAT LIFTED AN EYEBROW. His soft brown eyes narrowed into thin lines.

"Remove your hands from my sister." He spoke each word firmly, yet hardly above a whisper.

Ben's arm fell to his side. He stood and faced Nat. "Your sister was upset, Nathan. I only wished to comfort her."

"Your arm was around her."

"Yes, it was."

"You should have called me."

"I should have."

With those three words, Private Benjamin Clayton won my friendship and my respect, partly because of the way he protected Nat's honor, partly because he was kind and gentle. All Yankees were not the same.

Nat was not so easily swayed. "Then why did you not?"

Ben turned to me. "Elizabeth, may I speak to your brother in private?"

"Wait downstairs, Lizzie," Nat said.

They thought to send me below so they could have one of those men only conversations, unsuitable for a lady's ears, did they? They couldn't force me to go. I wouldn't. What if more deserters lurked in hidden places? Had Nat and Ben considered that? Obviously they hadn't. Even now, strange noises creaked and groaned below us.

"I searched the house, Lizzie," Nat said, anticipating my thoughts. "The Yankees are gone. They won't return." He placed a teacup with a chip on one side in my hand. "Your tea is cold. There's hot on the stove."

Nat was getting too big for his pants. Sometimes I doubly hated being a "fragile" girl, who was supposed to be polite and courteous and have no serious thoughts of my own, save to marry a good man and raise a passel of children. The unfairness of it all stuck in my throat. Nat escorted me to the kitchen, but I no longer desired tea.

"Stay out of the parlor, Lizzie," he said.

More orders. I went straight to the parlor and wished I hadn't. The destruction left by the Yankees sent me into a rage. I stomped around the room, calling them evil and vandals and deserters, and was glad I had shot Mack. Glad! No! I came to an abrupt standstill, horrified at the wicked thoughts racing through me.

I sank down on the floor, glass crunching underneath me. The problem of my feelings evaporated when I thought of Mama's dismay at seeing her favorite mirror in hundreds of pieces. I had to spare her that scene. The mirror was impossible to put back together, but I could tidy up the room and save some of Papa's and Willie's books. And if she asked about the empty frame, where the mirror had once been, I'd suggest a shell might have broken it. Someday, years from now, I'd tell her about Mack. If we survived. Choices were not easy; I hoped I was making the right one. I picked up slivers of glass. I unwrinkled pages of books. I was so busy I didn't notice Nat come in, until he took a stack of books from me and shelved them.

"Ben is going with us," he said, quite casually.

Nat called him Ben, a good sign. But I wasn't sure about the rest. "Going? Where?"

"To the moon."

Naturally. Where else? Private Clayton was indeed an extraordinary young man. He had made peace with Nat, no easy task. "You and Ben are friends then?" I asked.

Nat lifted his shoulders in an indifferent shrug, but his face lit up. "He's all right. He thinks you're charming."

"He does?" Never in my wildest dreams had I fancied a Yankee thinking me charming, or pretty, or any such thing. It made my insides warm and fluttery. Was this the same feeling that caused Mama's eyes to sparkle when Papa was around? I'd have to ask her.

"I told him you're fourteen."

My dream burst. I lashed out. "Near to fifteen, and I'm not stepping one foot on the moon, Nathan Stamford."

"Not even with Ben?"

Before I could slap him beside the head, Nat ran.

By the time Mama, Aunt Lois, and Uncle Morris returned from church, Nat and I were sitting without the mouth of the cave. I had written Ben's letter to his family and was penning one to Willie.

Mama peered over my shoulder. "Tell your brother to take care of himself," she said, "and we'll send Joseph and him reading material and the doctor's pocket knife. They may find a use for it."

Her mention of everyday things brought me a small measure of contentment. So much had happened this one long morning that I had begun to think it was only a dream, and I never shot anyone, and Ben had not put his arm around me. But I knew better. If I could start the day over, I would go to church with Mama rather than to the house. Then Mack would not be wounded, or dead, but Ben might be, had the deserters discovered him. What a tangled mess I was in. My conscience urged me to tell Mama about Mack; instead, I made small talk. "How was church?" I asked.

She let out a deep sigh, took off her bonnet, and plopped it on the table beside her rocking chair. "The Federals have no respect for Sunday or the Lord's house. Shells were a constant threat. Thank heavens you and Nathan were here and safe."

Nat got very busy, doing something. Biting his tongue, I imagine.

"Plaster and scraps of wood covered the pews and the floor," Mama went on. "We had to clean a place to sit. Few people attended, too frightened to leave the caves, I suppose. In spite of the sparse attendance, the minister delivered an inspiring message. Afterward, he requested volunteers to prepare lint and bandages. It seems we never have enough."

She dabbed at her eyes with her handkerchief. "We'll meet the Reverend and the other ladies at the church after lunch, honey, to lend a hand."

But Mama's words were a jumbled noise in my ears, for I had found stains on my dress. Blood. I crumpled up my skirt in a futile attempt to conceal them, which only drew Mama's attention.

She bent down and lifted my hand. "Elizabeth, honey. This is blood." Her sharp gaze scanned every inch of me. "Are you injured?" she asked.

I was finding it easier and easier to, if not outright lie, at least stretch the truth. I concluded it was better to tell a small fib than to make Mama worry. "My shoes are in pathetic condition, Mama. The sole on this one came loose, and I fell and scraped my elbow." I held my foot up to show her.

The first part was true: the sole hung by a slim thread. So I considered my words only a half-lie, which had to be better than a whole one, didn't it?

Nat made a funny noise. I shot him a warning look.

Mama was all gentle concern. "Let me see, honey." She commenced to roll up my sleeve.

I pulled out of her grasp and quickly pushed down my sleeve. "It's a tiny scrape, Mama. I already bandaged it."

She studied me a moment, as if debating whether to believe me or not. "I see." She flung her gloves on top of her bonnet. "This wretched war! The river blockade prevents us from buying even a decent pair of shoes. It's been so long since I've tasted ice cream, or lemonade, or cake that I scarcely recall their flavor. Whatever is to become of us? I shan't let you run around in your bare feet, Elizabeth, and make you the gossip of our neighbors. I'll sew you the finest pair of shoes you have ever owned."

"Without shoes Lizzie might stay out of trouble," Nat said.

His tone assured me he was furious that I had made him an accomplice to my storytelling. Oh, yes. I would have to answer for that someday. I wasn't proud of myself.

"Nathan! Bite your tongue, young man!" Mama said. "No respectable lady shows her feet or ankles."

"Lizzie has, when she went swimming with Joseph, Willie, Patrick, and me. Actually, we saw more than her feet."

Mama gasped. "You didn't! When was this, Nathan? Why are you just now telling me? What exactly did you see?"

"Her unmentionables," Nat said, looking at me smugly, getting his revenge.

I stuck out my tongue at him. "I couldn't swim in shoes, Mama," I said in my defense. "Or petticoats. I'd have sunk to the bottom. Besides, I'm not the only one. Miriam did, too. Willie was very attentive to her. Nat kept tickling her bare toes. Patrick said I looked nice."

"His actual word was 'scandalous,'" Nat said, correcting me.

My angry glares went right over Nat's head.

"We shall discuss your conduct later, Elizabeth." Mama took off her shawl. "Poor Patrick. He was a sweet boy and much too young to die. I must call on his parents and see how they are."

She wet her thumb, scraped at dirt on my face. "He was a perfect beau for you, Elizabeth. A true gentleman. He'd have made a lady of you."

"Patrick?" Nat and I said at the same time. Mama did not know him the way we knew him.

"I'll get to your shoes this evening, honey," Mama said. "Until then, try to walk lightly."

"Yes, Mama."

After lunch we gathered our old linen and cotton rags and petticoats, which I was happy to donate to the cause, and returned to the church. Though the mortars fired hot and heavy all afternoon, we shut our ears to the sounds and made bandages and lint. I preferred my guitar and books to the chatter of the other ladies, but consoled myself with the fact that the Yankee, Ben, was improving. Our bandages might make a difference in some other soldier's life. Near twilight, exhausted, hot, and sweaty, we trudged back to the cave, satisfied that we had helped the war in our own small way.

By candlelight, I commenced to write Willie's letter:

May 24, 1863, Sunday

Dearest Brother Willie,

Mama says to take care. I echo her words. I've seen
what the Yankees can do. This morning, I met the
meanest Yankee you ever imagined. I shot him, Willie,
which makes me blue. But I had to protect Nat and
Ben. Let me explain about Ben.

I found him under a tree, wounded. At first I
thought to shoot him. (Ben's a Yankee, but not mean).
Then I put you and Joseph in his place and could not.
So he's in my room. Nat wasn't fond of the Yankee at
first. Now they're friends.

Please write. We've had no word from you in weeks.
Do the Yankees control the mail like everything else?
Just a thought. Mama says the star pin she gave you
will keep you safe. I pray for you and Joseph to come
home soon.

                              Love you always,
                              Lizzie

I sealed the letter in an envelope. This was my last sheet of paper. Should the war drag on much longer, I'd be reduced to writing
on the back of letters Willie and Joseph sent, or on wallpaper, the
way James M. Swords, editor of *The Daily Citizen*, was printing his
newspaper.

Later, I sat beside Nat outside the cave and watched the flames
of light scatter across the sky, such a lovely sight to cause such horrible destruction.

"Go home, Yankees," I whispered.

I knew they would not.

Chapter 16

THE MORNING STRETCHED BEFORE ME, long and dreary. I hardly knew what to do with myself. I opened *Sonnets from the Portuguese*, but Elizabeth Barrett Browning's poetry blurred before my eyes. I read from Charles Dickens. His words gave me no solace. My head swirled with unbidden remembrances. Mack's face, contorted with pain and hate, was painted in my memory, for eternity. Private Arnold, the others.... Such sadness their families must endure. I yearned to receive a note from my brothers, to know they were well. Though the morning was already hot, I shivered. I put down my book and gathered my shawl about me.

Aunt Lois hummed softly as she mixed something in a kettle. I cared little what it was. My appetite had flown. Ben raised many questions in my mind, mostly about our servants. Was Aunt Lois truly happy, cooking and cleaning and caring for my brothers and me? She had no children of her own, so we were her family. Were we enough? Was she pleased with her life, or would she prefer her own home, just Uncle Morris and her? To add more puzzlement to my already bewildered mind, my thoughts jumped from our servants to Ben. My stomach fluttered, as if hundreds of butterflies were flapping their wings inside me. I must be in love. And with a Yankee. Oh my!

Nat's voice interrupted my rambling brain. "Uncle Morris is busy, so Mother asked me to take Ben his lunch," he said. "Want to come along? Mother gives her permission, so long as you stay with me."

"Do I?" He didn't have to ask twice.

I started one direction, but Nat went another. "You're going the wrong way," I said.

"I want to pay a visit to the courthouse first to see the gunboats."

"You'd let Ben's lunch get cold so you can watch a bunch of boats floating on the river?"

He grinned and his legs moved faster.

I panted to keep up with his long strides. "You're hopeless, Nat."

"You've told me that before."

Save for a couple of Confederate soldiers and a straggler or two, the courthouse, sitting high atop a hill, was deserted.

"Let's climb to the top," Nat said.

I was anxious to see Ben, but Nat was already ascending the stairs to the balcony around the cupola of the courthouse. Though I found nothing exciting about some ugly old boats, I trailed after him and had to admit the view from this height was magnificent. In the sunlight, the hills sparkled, yellow with grain, peaceful and calm. Were we invincible, the way some people believed, impregnable because our clay bluffs were too well fortified to capture? Sometimes looks were deceiving. A glance at the clumps of trees to the east, where white smoke revealed the location of Federal cannon, painted a more accurate picture. Vicksburg was under siege, from both land and water. We were not invincible. In fact, in my opinion, we were very vulnerable. I descended the stairs. I had seen enough.

⁊ʘʘʘ

Ben was sitting on the porch steps when we arrived at the house.

"Elizabeth. Nathan." He rose, reached out to take my hand, and almost fell on his face.

Men! Why did they refuse to admit it when they were ill? "What do you think you're doing, Ben?" I asked. "You're weak as a kitten, yet here you are on the porch, in the open, for every passerby to see, for every soldier to use for target practice."

He accepted my reproof with a straightening of his spine. "Thank you for your concern, Elizabeth, but I have caused you enough trouble. I shall take my leave now."

He took a tottering step.

"You'll do nothing of the kind, Benjamin Clayton," I said, the way I'd reprimand Nat, should he be so insolent. "Papa will decide when you're well enough to take your leave. It's back to bed with you now. No arguments."

Ben seemed to have a stubborn streak to equal that of the Stamfords. "Each day I stay in your home brings danger to you and your family, Elizabeth. If the Rebels discover me, they'll consider you traitors for providing shelter to the enemy. Sometimes they imprison traitors or even shoot them, I think."

"You do have much to learn, Ben. Nobody is going to shoot us. Papa's a doctor. His hospital shelters both Yankee and Confederate wounded."

"Don't misunderstand me, Elizabeth. I appreciate you and your father taking me in, attending my wounds, but I don't plan to spend the war in prison, which is where your father will send me."

I had no arguments to convince him otherwise. I didn't want him in prison either. My girlish dreams vanished like the morning mist. This War Between the States was not about states, but about people, people who had no say in their own lives. I looked up into his eyes. "Will we see you again, Ben?"

"I should like to call on you, Elizabeth," he said quite serious, "with your permission and your mother's and father's blessings."

Right then I'd have given anything for a fan to hide my blush. Since one was not available, I had to settle for lowered lashes and hoped Ben didn't notice. He might have, save that Nat thrust the basket of food at him. Sometimes Nat intruded at the right time.

"You can't go before you eat," Nat said, his voice husky. "We brought you cornbread and soup. Don't ask what's in it. Aunt Lois says it's her secret recipe."

"It smells delicious." Ben offered Nat a hand. They shook in friendship.

I swear Nat grew inches taller. He had never had a true friend, which endeared Ben to me even more.

Ben sat on the steps and ate like a man starving, yet with an air of dignity I found delightful. When scarcely a crumb was left, he wiped his sleeve across his mouth. "Give Aunt Lois my compliments, Nathan. Tell her I look forward to meeting her someday."

"She'll be pleased," Nat said.

Ben stood, the food having given him strength. He pulled an envelope out of his pocket. "I almost forgot. The courier came by earlier with a dispatch for you, Elizabeth. I told him I'd see that you got it."

I recognized the broad, bold script at once. I was so excited I'm afraid I acted quite shamefully. I threw my arms around his neck and cried, "Thank you, Ben, thank you."

He coughed. Realizing what I had done, I quickly released him, but didn't regret the hug.

"No thanks are called for, Elizabeth," he said. "I only delivered the message."

My hands held the long-awaited letter from Willie. I ripped open the envelope and giggled with delight at the first thing I saw—a drawing of a girl playing the piano. "To Elizabeth, with love, Joseph," was scribbled underneath it. I held the drawing for Nat and Ben to see.

Ben chuckled. "Joseph is a talented artist. He captured your image perfectly, down to that wild straggle of hair in your eye."

"Even better, this letter proves that Joseph and Willie are alive and well."

Ben gave Nat a second envelope. "This one is addressed to your father," he said.

"For Papa?" I asked. "Is it from Joseph?" A letter from both brothers would delight Mama and Papa.

Nat scanned the writing. "The name is unfamiliar to me."

With a look, Ben and Nat communicated in that odd way they had developed in the short time they had known each other. "I'll stay with Elizabeth while you deliver it," Ben said.

Nat hurried off. I made myself comfortable on the steps and continued reading:

Virginia, Late April or May
(Never can recall the date. Ask Joseph.)

Dear Lizzie Tizzie,

I grinned. Willie called me Lizzie Tizzie, his special name for me for as long as I could remember. He was in good spirits. Or so I thought, until I read on:

> I was going to tell you what great experiences I'm having, but Father taught us to speak the truth. So I'll tell you like it is. I never expected to feel so helpless when seeing a friend shot down before my eyes, like I should do something, only I cannot. For the first time since I enlisted, I realize it could happen to me. Or to Joseph. That, Lizzie Tizzie, is a sobering awakening.
>
> But I shan't burden your ears with my mad musings. I miss you and Mother and Father and little Nathan. Sometimes I'm afraid I shall never see you again. It helps that Joseph and I are together.
>
> We talk, mostly about home. Home. What a delightful word. I little appreciated it when I was there. How oft I think of it now.
>
> It disturbs me that Joseph wishes for Mississippi to remain part of the Union. We quarrel about that some. Friendly-like. Joseph has a way of convincing you he is right, save on this matter I strongly disagree. I quote from the great Patrick Henry: "I know not what course others may take, but as for me, give me liberty or give me death." Braver words I have never heard spoken.
>
> Say, Lizzie, I found four hairs on my chin. Joseph is growing whiskers. He wants to look like Father. But I shan't have the girls see me hairy as a bear. Please send me a razor in your next letter. Tell Mother and Father I'll drop them a few lines tonight.

Joseph sends his love, will write later. Our health is good. Nothing more to say.

Brother Willie

A lump formed in my throat. Willie's earlier letters had been full of fun. He had described the lands they passed through, the soldiers, the food, but this one was different. My happy-go-lucky, life-is-an-adventure brother sounded terribly lonesome. Was that what it was like to be far away from family and friends? No mother to smooth your pillow, to kiss away your hurts. No father to give words of praise and guide you through the dark moments.

"You look distressed," Ben said. "Bad news?"

"Bad? No. Yes. Willie's homesick."

Ben eased down next to me. He clasped his hands on his knees. "I know the feeling. I have no brothers and sisters. My mother and father are growing old. I'm all they have. Should I not return what will they do?"

I only said to Ben what I'd have told Willie. "One day the cannon will cease firing, the mortars will hush their growling, and you, my friend, will find yourself in Ohio. Your mother and father will throw you a party. The girls will flock around you, their hero."

I whispered a prayer that it might be true, save for the last part. Leave out the girls.

"You do know how to make a fellow feel better," Ben said. "Your brothers are lucky to have you for their sister." He tilted his head. "As for the girls you mentioned, I have nobody special. Would you take pity on a poor lonesome soul and write to me?"

No special girl, no special girl rang like music in my ears. Without thinking, as usual, I blurted out, "Every day."

My impulsive tongue had done it again. He'd think me no lady. For the first time in my life, I cared to be a lady, to please Ben. "I mean...." I hushed. Anything I said would make matters worse.

When he smiled, I melted.

"I'll await your letters with eagerness, Elizabeth. Every day."

Amid the roar and thunder of gunfire, the shells, and death, I had found a beautiful friendship to treasure. Perhaps someday....

The iron gate at the end of the sidewalk squeaked, as Nat pushed through it. My greeting never passed my lips, for he laid his head on my lap. He said only one word: "Lizzie."

Chapter 17

N AT WAS SO LIMP I thought he had fainted. Lightly, I touched his hair. "Nat?"

He slowly raised his head.

His eyes.... I had no words to describe the emptiness, the look of despair I beheld in his eyes. Something horrible must have happened when he delivered the letter to Papa. My imagination leapt to the worst conclusions. "Nat! It's Papa, isn't it? He's hurt." I bounded up, sending Nat tumbling. "We must go to him."

Nat struggled to his feet. "Father's all right. The letter... it... Lizzie."

Icy fingers of dread clutched at my throat. "Something in the letter?"

Nat sank to his knees, cupped his face in his hands. I knelt before him, pried his fingers open. "What are you trying to tell me, Nat? What was in the letter?"

"It said...." A ragged wheeze shook his body. It took him a moment to find his voice. "Lizzie, Father's on his w-way to the c-cave."

Nat's announcement paralyzed me with fear. "Mama's ill?"

"No. She's... Father's...."

I could stand his stumbling attempt at comprehensible words no longer. "Talk to me, Nat! What did the letter say?"

Ben reached out and rested his hand on Nat's shoulder. "Take a deep breath, Nathan."

Nat squared his back, gulped in air.

"Good," Ben said. "Another."

Nat breathed longer, deeper. The ashen gray of his face returned to a near normal color.

"Now, Nathan," Ben said gently. "What was in the letter to your father?"

"Willie...." Nat's face crumpled. Great sobs ripped from his throat. He put his head against my cheek. "Willie... he's...."

Willie? "No!" I wrenched away from Nat and fled.

I tore down the street and through a stand of trees, scratching my arms on the low branches, hearing my dress rip, hardly noticing. Or caring. Screams wailed in my ears. Mine? Footfalls drummed behind me. Closer. Closer. My legs were near to falling off. My lungs burned. I felt pressure on my arm, and Ben was there, hugging me to him, stroking my hair, murmuring softly, "I'm sorry, Elizabeth. So very sorry."

I shook my head. "It's a mistake. A cruel mistake. I have Willie's letter. I have his letter. I have his...."

"Stop it, Lizzie!" Nat stood behind Ben.

I hiccupped, gulped, grasped at a slim thread of hope. "Willie wrote me, Nat. See." I flapped his letter in the air.

Nat held out a hand. "Come over here, Lizzie."

In a daze of disbelief, I shuffled over, and he tucked me under his arm. "I want you out of my house, Yankee," Nat said. His jaw danced. "Now."

"I expected you would," Ben said. "Nathan, in spite of what you believe, I am sorry about your brother, and I am your friend." To me he added, "I'm here for you, Elizabeth, whatever you need. Just ask."

"She doesn't need, or want, anything from you, Yankee," Nat said, his words laced with bitterness.

In a foggy corner of my brain I heard Ben reply, unintelligible words that fell away. I don't recall Ben leaving. I don't remember walking to the cave, where I sank into Mama's lap, my head on her soft breast. In the stillness of our underground home, she rocked me, as tenderly as she had when I was a baby. Papa's arms encircled us. People dropped by all afternoon. Neighbors. Friends. Strangers. They brought food. No one ate. Voices droned on and on, like a hive of busy bumblebees, until I thought I'd go crazy. My mind kept repeating, "It's a mistake, someone else, not our Willie," and I clung to that thought.

General Pemberton came to call, but Mama, unable to face another word of sympathy, retired with her regrets to her dark room
behind the curtain. I sat with her, and listened to the general and
Papa talking.

"Your tragedy touches me deeply, Charles," General Pemberton
said. "Your son was a brave soldier."

"William is ... was a fine young man," Papa said, a hint of pride
in his voice.

"Willie," I said, remembering. Willie winking at the girls. Willie chasing Nat through the trees. Willie reading, late at night. He
was impetuous, like me, and seldom thought before acting. Once
he went to the river and threw Joseph's new boots into the water because Joseph had made Willie angry about something—the
particular incident escapes me now. Whatever the reason, Joseph
and Willie scuffled and fell into the Mississippi. That's when Nat
decided to see if a person could live underwater like a fish. Had
Willie not pulled him out, Nat would have drowned. Now those
days were gone forever.

Papa and General Pemberton chatted awhile longer, and then
Pemberton said, "I'll take my leave now, Charles. I sent a flag of
truce to General Grant, requesting a cease-fire to bury the dead. He
has agreed."

The soldiers, buried where they fell, their families unaware of
their final resting place. Ben's greatest fear, he had said. I attempted
to say a prayer for him, but could not. I prayed for Willie to appear
and put to rest the rumors of his death. I wouldn't believe it, but
inside, I knew.

After the general left, Papa came to see about Mama, so I went
outside. A truce meant a time without shells flying through the air.
I wandered about aimlessly, no particular destination in mind, but
soon found myself at the house, the last place I had seen Willie before he enlisted in the army. The leaves of the giant oak tree at the
side of the house whispered in the breeze, inviting—Willie's tree
and mine, our secret place. We would sit in its twisted branches

for hours and talk and dream, or else we would hide from Mama and Papa when we had committed a punishable offense. I could picture Willie now, grinning wickedly from the upper branches, bidding me to join him. I shinnied up the rough trunk and perched in the spot Willie claimed was his. Willie's presence surrounded me, warmed me. He would tell me to stand tall and strong, like the tree. Like Willie. Brave thoughts. Impossible thoughts. Whatever made a person courageous was missing in me. I was like the soft moss that grows on the trees, clinging to something else for support—Mama, Papa, even Nat.

"I see you, Lizzie." Quicker than a squirrel, Nat scampered up the tree and balanced on the branch below me.

I had expected him. If I traveled to the ends of the earth Nat would find me. I leaned against the tree trunk. Part of me wanted to be alone to nurse my sorrow and to pray for a miracle. Part of me desired Nat's company. As if I had a choice.

"I hurt inside, Lizzie," he said.

All day he had kept to himself, grieving in his own quiet way. I had been so selfish in my misery that I had forgotten he lost a brother, the same as me. I scooted down and held him to me. "I know, Nat. I know. My insides are hollow, like somebody took a knife and cut out all the good things inside me."

His lower lip quivered. "You still have Joseph and me, Lizzie. We're very nice brothers. You have Mother and Father. Aunt Lois and Uncle Morris."

Poor Nat. He meant well, but my heart was too heavy to appreciate the family I had. I could only think of the one I lost. "But not Willie. He ought to have stayed home, Nat, with us. Then he'd be alive. Why did he have to go?"

Nat wriggled out of my grasp. He stripped bark off the tree, shredded it, giving himself time to consider my question. Finally, he pointed to a branch higher up. "Look above you, Lizzie."

What a strange request. I couldn't imagine what the tree had to do with Willie, or the rest of us for that matter, but Nat seldom did anything without good cause. I raised myself up and peered between a clump of leaves. A bird's nest was nestled in the fork of a slender tree branch. Three heads stretched up, and three yellow mouths opened wide. Three baby birds, covered with wispy fuzz, thought I was their mother, bringing them dinner.

Nat said nothing more, but his message was clear. The birds were young and helpless, dependent on their mother to provide their needs, if only for a short while. Soon they would fly away to explore the world, and their mother would have to hope they survived the perils awaiting them, the way Mama was doing now, with her children. The difference was the mother bird would never know her babies' fate. Mama did. And I ought to be with her.

Nat gave me a hand down from the tree.

As we picked our way through the scattered shrapnel and shell fragments that littered the street, I kept thinking of General Pemberton's men burying the soldiers in the field. No markers would identify them. Grass would cover the graves. Everyone would forget them and the reason they had given their lives. Was that to be Willie's fate? I had to know. Nat had been with Papa when he read the letter. Perhaps it said.

"Nat, did they put a stone on Willie's grave? Did Joseph tell them his name? Is Joseph well?"

"You can ask him in a few days. They're coming home."

They. I had my answer.

Chapter 18

TIME SEEMED TO MOVE SLOWER than a hot summer day. I counted the hours, minutes, seconds until Joseph's return. Willie was harder to think about. At least he would be home, rather than lying under soil we knew not where. We could visit with him, tell him we love him, and Nat would bring flowers for his grave. But it would only be a shell of our brother, a memory, not the flesh and blood living one I longed to see and touch and laugh with.

On Wednesday morning, 2 days, 48 hours, 2,880 minutes after receiving our heartbreaking news, Nat and I were sitting without the cave, playing chess and scanning every face that passed by, in hopes the next person would be Joseph, when several ladies crossed the ravine and hastened in the direction of the river.

"What's happening?" Nat called.

"Federal gunboats are attacking our batteries!" one lady called back.

"Come on, Lizzie!" Nat was up and off.

Another battle on the river was nothing unusual, but for want of anything better to do, and since I wished not to be alone, I trailed after him.

At Sky Parlor Hill, a distance of two squares from the river and the highest place in Vicksburg, where the Mississippi was visible for miles, I beheld five gunboats at one end of the river. A monster-sized boat, the *Cincinnati*, Nat told me, lay farther upstream. As I watched, a shot from our cannon cut away the flagpole of the boat. Another struck her in the side, and a third hit her above the waterline. Severely damaged, she steamed back up the river. The dark waters boiled in her wake.

"She's going down!" Nat cried, caught up in the insanity with the rest of the crowd.

The *Cincinnati* sank near the shore. To avoid the same fate, the other boats retreated. Near to a hundred ladies who witnessed our army's victory waved their handkerchiefs and shouted cheers.

"We won, Lizzie!" Nat said with enthusiasm. "The Yankees are running!"

Everyone was absolutely giddy with the outcome of the battle, but I wondered about the men on board the boat. How many were there? Had any survived? I thought I saw a man hanging onto a bale of hay, floating in the water close by the *Cincinnati*. Without a glass to look through, it was hard to tell. Whether he drowned or was rescued mattered little to me. The sailors were Yankees, which should bring me satisfaction. It did not.

Nat grabbed me up and twirled me around until I was breathless. "We beat 'em, Lizzie," he said. "A victory for Willie."

"Too late for Willie."

"He knows," Nat said.

Nat was so confident I hadn't the heart to spoil his joy.

The battle was over, at least for the present, so we descended the wooden steps on the street side of the hill. Why we chose to return to the house, instead of the cave, will forever remain a mystery. Perhaps because of our triumph on the river and our thoughts of Willie, we forgot the present and went back to an earlier, happier time. Whatever brought on our temporary lapse of memory, I am thankful, for the most pleasant surprise awaited us.

೮つ೮ろ

Tall and good-looking, though thinner than when last I saw him, he stood before us. His gray jacket was ragged and soiled. His haversack hung carelessly over his shoulder, and he clutched a musket tightly in his hand. He leaned on a stick, serving as a crude, makeshift crutch. My gaze lingered on his leg. I winced at the sight of his pants, stiff with what appeared to be mud, but most likely was dried blood. Underneath the cloth, which was cut from his hip to his ankle, a filthy bandage needed replacing. I could do that.

He let his haversack and musket fall to the floor and limped toward me, that Stamford smile lighting up his eyes. He moved so slowly I thought he should never reach me, so I hurled myself into his arms. "Joseph!"

He buried his face in my hair. Warm tears dampened my scalp. "Lizzie. Thank God you're all right. When I saw the house...." He held me out, appraised me all the way from my toes to my head. "You're still the prettiest girl in Vicksburg," he said, his voice deep, husky.

"And you are still the handsomest man in Vicksburg." I folded my arms about his waist, wanting never to let go. Joseph was home, alive. In the darkest corner of my mind, I wept for the brother who was not, whose pulse no longer beat.

Nat circled Joseph, giving him a thorough examination. "You're wounded, brother. How?"

Joseph closed his eyes, as though to drive away some vision only he could see. He spoke, his voice heavy, halting. "Willie saved my life."

"You were together then," I said. "When...." The words refused to pass my lips.

Joseph opened his eyes and ran his hand through his hair. "We were together."

He fumbled in his pocket, dug out a piece of metal, and laid it in my palm. His Adam's apple bobbed up and down when he swallowed. "Willie wanted you to have this, Lizzie. His last words were for you." Joseph's voice took on a prayerful reverence that, for a moment, silenced even the sounds of war. "'I'll always be with you, Lizzie, in spirit, if not in body,' Willie said. He....'"

Joseph looked down at his feet.

Willie's star pin, lying cold in my hand, removed any lingering doubts I had the letter was mistaken. An incredible sadness rushed through me, and I gripped the pin in my fist. Pain squeezed at my chest. How barbaric was war. But Joseph had been there, too. He might have.... I cut off that thought. God had spared Joseph, for He knew we could not have borne the loss of both brothers.

I rested my hand on the rough stubble of whiskers on his face. "You're home, Joseph. That's all that matters. You brought Willie. I have my brothers back."

"I could not leave him to lie among strangers," Joseph said. "He ought to be with family."

Joseph unfastened the pin on his shirt, uncurled my fingers, and placed it with Willie's. "You can have mine, too. They brought us no luck."

I had never heard such bitterness, worse even than Nat. "How can you say that, Joseph? You're home, safe."

He snorted. "What's left of me is here. Or haven't you noticed my leg?"

I detected a note of self-pity in his voice that greatly disturbed me. Sharp words of reproof sprang to the tip of my tongue, but I choked them back. Joseph had suffered much, poor tortured soul, but he couldn't let what happened destroy him. Nor could I. This war robbed me of one brother. It caused another brother to grow up too fast. We lost friends. I wouldn't allow Joseph to be another victim. He had to put the past behind him and look ahead. I smiled wryly to myself. I should listen to my own advice.

I offered words of encouragement. "Papa is an excellent surgeon, Joseph. He'll heal your leg."

"He can perform miracles?"

Ignore the sarcasm. "He does. All the time."

"How bad is the leg?" Nat asked.

"Bad enough to muster me out of the army. I'll carry this limp the rest of my life." Joseph's shoulders slumped. He muttered under his breath. "I wish the bullet had found its mark. It should have been me, instead of Willie. It should have been me."

Clearly Joseph's injuries went deeper than his leg. He blamed himself for the loss of Willie, which was crazy. No two brothers were more devoted to each other. Whatever had occurred in Virginia, Joseph was not at fault. The wounds of his body would heal; I wasn't so sure about the wounds within. But I would do whatever necessary to make him whole again.

I leaned in to kiss his face. "Welcome home, Joseph." Then softer I said, "Welcome home, Willie."

Nat had some healing techniques of his own. He retrieved Joseph's musket, threw his haversack over his own shoulder, slipped his arm in the curve of Joseph's elbow, and guided him toward the door. "Remember the time you and Willie chased the mule into Mother's flower garden," Nat said, "and the mule decided roses were its favorite food. By the time Mother discovered the disaster, every petal was eaten, along with the thorns."

Joseph's face crinkled in a question. "How do you know about that? You were just a baby."

"Lizzie told me."

I lifted my shoulders in a helpless shrug. "It was his favorite nighttime story. Put him to sleep every time."

That easily Nat drew Joseph away from whatever ghosts were tormenting him, for a while.

ଚଔ

Papa was standing at the entrance of the cave, staring into space, his hands folded behind his back, when we arrived. The next minutes were hectic, crazy, and deliriously happy and sad when he ran to Joseph and gathered him in his arms. Mama wept when Joseph embraced her. Joseph said very little. No one insisted. He was so fragile I think we were scared he would retreat inside himself to somewhere we couldn't reach, and we would lose him, too.

That evening Aunt Lois cooked a special meal in honor of Joseph, as special as she could manage, considering our limited resources. Papa had procured some beef from a cow that had roamed into the line of fire. *The one I encountered earlier?* We had fresh fruit that Nat foraged from somewhere. Joseph ate hardly anything. He listened to our chatter, but volunteered nothing. Papa kept shaking his head at me when I started to question Joseph, a silent warning to give him time. So whenever a thought popped into my brain, I stuffed a bite of food in my mouth to prevent me from airing my unending comments and questions. They all were grateful, I suppose. I ate like a field hand, which delighted Aunt Lois, who always fussed at me for eating like a bird. I don't know where she got that idea. The birds I observed ate huge amounts.

After supper, I was helping Aunt Lois with the dishes, and Nat was showing Joseph the plans for his flying machine in an attempt to make conversation with him, when a man rushed up to the cave yelling, "Dr. Stamford, Dr. Stamford, come quick!"

Papa grabbed his medical bag and left with the man. Our curiosity aroused, Nat and I followed. In a large cave carved into the hillside not far from ours, where two, perhaps three, families were living, a baby was being born. Soon a high-pitched mewl blended with the sound of hissing and screeching shells. It reminded me of a kitten mewing for its mother. A strong, lusty yowl when Papa laid a wrinkled, pink-faced baby in its mother's arms made everybody laugh.

"It's a girl!" the proud father exclaimed. He named her Hope.

After many thanks from the mother and father, we went home to report the addition of Vicksburg's newest citizen to Mama and Joseph.

Later, Nat settled beside me on my mattress, where I was attempting to read by candlelight, with little success. Too many thoughts pattered about in my mind, but Nat brought them to a jolting halt.

"Lizzie, is it always so painful to have a baby?"

Caught completely off my guard I cried, "Great granny's pantalets! What a question!"

"Well, is it?"

The same thought had occurred to me, though I'd never admit it to anyone, especially my brother. Ladies were not supposed to think of such things. I shut my book and answered honestly. "You're asking the wrong person, Nat. What I know about babies would fill a thimble. Ask Mama."

"She's with Joseph, behind the curtain. I won't disturb them."

"Is this a secret meeting?" Papa asked. "Or am I invited."

"Father," Nat said. "You'll do."

Papa raised an eyebrow. "I will? I appreciate your confidence, son. What is the deep discussion? What can I 'do'?"

"Tell me about babies."

Papa flicked me a look. I lowered my lashes, but my ears listened in anticipation.

"Very well, Nathan, but one doesn't discuss such delicate matters in a lady's presence."

"Outside then?" Nat asked.

I crept after them and eavesdropped shamelessly, my cheeks burning the whole time.

That night, I dreamed of Ben and wondered where he was. Was he dreaming of me?

Chapter 19

AFTER WE LAID WILLIE TO REST, Mama busied herself making bandages, cartridges, and socks for our soldiers. Papa spent hours at the hospital, mending arms and legs and broken spirits. He attended to Joseph's leg, mumbled a lot, but assured Joseph it would heal. It was too bad he could not promise the same for Joseph's disagreeable disposition. At night, when we reminisced about Willie, recalling the little things about him—how he combed his hair just so, how he ironed his own shirts to give Aunt Lois a rest, how he encouraged me to read and learn about the world so he and I could travel to far and exotic countries someday—Joseph would leave. He would stay gone for hours, sometimes. But those evenings were precious to me. I could almost sense Willie's presence, as though he were listening and chuckling at his escapades along with us.

Now Willie and I would never go on those glorious adventures. He would never shave. He would forever be seventeen. I had good days and bad, days when I thought I couldn't go on. We all did, Joseph especially. He had no peace. In sleep, he whimpered and moaned, unable to escape his ghosts. He awoke with sweat drenching his thin body. Each day he withdrew more and more into himself, holding his sorrow inside. I hadn't the faintest idea how to ease his suffering. Even Nat, who was so much like Joseph, could not reach him.

One day when I was sweeping the carpet in the cave, which seemed a waste of time to me but Mama insisted, I accidentally knocked over my guitar. A string popped loose. As was my habit, I carried the guitar to my brother for repairs. Joseph was hunkered down on the ground, outside the cave, snapping twigs into splinters. "Joseph, my guitar string broke," I said. "Will you fix it for me?"

Normally he would tease me with something like "Strong-fingered Lizzie does it again" and have my guitar as good as new in less than two minutes. Now he just gave me that blank look. I'm not even certain he saw me. He lived in a world of his own making, letting no one in, nor letting himself out. Perhaps he was better off in that other place. Perhaps his memories were too horrid to bear. Despairing at my failure to get his attention, I rose. I sat back down. What kind of sister was I to abandon him? Whether he admitted it or not, Joseph needed us. We needed him. Eventually, if a fly is pesky enough, the person it's pestering takes note. I was that fly. I had no illusions it would be easy, but he had to face his ghosts, whatever they were, and make peace with them. And I was the girl to see that he did. So I gave it another try.

I pulled his star pin off my dress. "I polished your pin, Joseph. See how it sparkles. I'll put it on your shirt. I'm wearing Willie's. He would want you to...."

Joseph clumped to his feet—his leg was stiff and difficult for him to bend—and stumbled off, leaving my words hanging. At least I had accomplished one thing; he had noticed me. I started after him, determined to break through that wall he had built around himself.

But Nat came out just then. "Let him go, Lizzie. He wishes to be alone, to think. He'll come back."

"Are you sure? He's been thinking for days now, Nat, and he's only getting worse. What if he wanders off one day and encounters Yankees? He's hardly strong enough to defend himself. Or a bullet might strike him and send him tumbling into a ditch, wounded, unable to call for help."

A shadow of doubt flitted over Nat's face, quickly faded. "Joseph will be home by dark," he said. "He always is."

I wasn't as confident as Nat was.

At sunset, I squinted into the gathering dusk to catch sight of Joseph. There he comes. But no, it was another man. The minutes dragged by. My imagination ran wild: Joseph in the hands of Yankees, Joseph bleeding, Joseph crying out in pain, too far away for us to hear. When I couldn't stand it any longer, I tossed on my shawl.

"I'm going to find him," I told Mama and Nat.

All afternoon Mama had been as fidgety as a girl in a tight corset. She had sewed and read and rocked and sewed some more, as if she sensed something wrong. I expected her to object to my leaving the cave after dark and was surprised when she consented.

She smoothed my shawl around my shoulders. "Keep an eye out for your father, too, honey. I sent him a note an hour or so ago, thinking Joseph might have gone to the hospital. Your father hasn't replied, which is most unlike him."

She turned to Nat and straightened his collar. "Go with your sister, Nathan. Try the house first. Joseph may be confused and believe we're still living there."

"We will, Mother," Nat said.

But our house was empty.

"Perhaps a neighbor?" I said.

We went from door-to-door throughout the practically deserted neighborhood. We peered in broken windows and entered un-locked houses. We called, "Joseph."

I asked a couple of our soldiers on the road, "Have you seen a young Confederate, walking with a limp? He's tall, blond."

"Only every day," one said with a sigh.

"We'll watch for him," the other soldier promised.

"We'd best return to the cave, Lizzie," Nat said when we had looked everyplace possible, "lest Mother sends Uncle Morris after us. Anyway, Joseph is probably there by now."

The thought had crossed my mind. Reluctantly, I agreed. I picked up my skirt, and we hastened over shell fragments and torn up earth. As we crossed the ravine at the foot of the hill, a strange sound drifted out of the darkness. I stopped and gripped Nat's arm.

"Nat."

"I hear it, Lizzie. Somebody's singing."

"Bellowing is more like it. Nat, is that who I think it is?"

"Sure sounds like him."

Our heads turned, as one. Papa and Joseph were struggling to keep their balance on the sloping ground. Joseph sagged against

Papa, and they were singing at the top of their voices. Several people, attracted by the music, which was quite a change from our usual serenade of buzzing minie balls and clattering parrott shells, appeared from the yawning mouths of the caves.

Joseph waved. "Halloo!" he shouted, his words slurred. His head bobbed at Nat and me. He grinned. "Hey, Nathan, Lizzie Tizzie."

He took a step toward us and crumpled in a heap. Papa lifted him tenderly and carried him to his mattress in the cave.

Nat bent over Joseph. "What's wrong with him? What's that smell?"

"I believe he is somewhat tight," I said.

Nat's eyes got wide. "You mean drunk? Joseph?"

"After what he's been through, the boy is entitled," Papa said. "A drink or two chases away the phantoms. I almost indulged myself." He lowered his voice. "Your mother frowns on such behavior. She'll forgive her son, but hold her husband to blame forever."

Mama removed Joseph's boots. "Under the circumstances, you might have had a small drink, Charles," she said.

Papa chuckled. "I doubt you mean that, Susan." He smoothed back Joseph's hair. "He'll sleep easy tonight. He hasn't in a long while."

Mama, Papa, Nat, and I took turns watching over him throughout the night.

∽◯◌

The shells fell constantly with little reprieve, making our tempers short. Nat and I squabbled over the tiniest things, like what color were Hope's eyes? Did it matter? What was Nat's latest carving? Who cared? What day of the week was it? I had lost count. To be honest, I did the fussing. Nat usually gave in and agreed with me, which annoyed me more. Why couldn't he be grumpy once in a while, rather than shrugging off our living conditions, as if they were a minor irritation instead of a major catastrophe? And every attempt we made to communicate with Joseph ended in a dismal failure. His leg was improving; his disposition was not. Neither was mine, as Nat reminded me countless times.

Through it all, Mama watched us with thoughtful eyes and words of encouragement. "Give Joseph time," she said whenever I complained, "and love him."

"I try, Mama, but sometimes I don't even like him, so how can I love him?"

"Have patience, honey," she said.

"Patience," I reminded myself a hundred times a day.

We heard reports that a mortar shell had killed a young girl while she slept. Nat took wildflowers to the parents. They were the only kind left in Vicksburg, and they were scraggly and pathetic, like the rest of the town. This tragedy revealed how shallow and unimportant Nat's and my arguments were. He brought me a yellow bloom of some sort, possibly a weed, as a peace offering.

"I'm sorry, Lizzie," he said.

"Me, too," I said. "The flower's beautiful."

Our quarrels ceased, most of the time.

⋙⋘

One sultry June afternoon, Nat challenged me to a game of chess. Considering he was an expert and seldom lost, and I hardly knew a knight from a king or queen or pawn, I should have refused. But I was bored, and the slim possibility existed I might win. Very slim, I soon discovered. Three games later I admitted defeat. "You're too good for me," I said. "Joseph taught you well. He's the only one who ever whips you."

Nat and I looked at each other, the same thought flashing in both our minds. He plucked up the chess set and carried it to where Joseph was sitting, gazing at nothing. We planted ourselves on either side of him. He never moved. His indifference didn't divert us one bit. We commenced setting up the chessmen. Once they were in place, I raised an eyebrow at Nat and mouthed, "Now?"

He nodded.

Since Joseph was staring straight ahead, I leaned around to peer into his face. For an instant, I beheld my old Joseph. Then his expression changed, and he was again the stranger, who only bore an outward resemblance to my brother. But my Joseph was in that body; I had caught a glimpse of him. I would bring him out, one way or the other. Be patient, I told myself.

"Joseph, I have a problem," I said. "Nat always wins at chess, which makes him quite arrogant. Would you please teach me how to anticipate his moves so that, just once, I can whip him? You be white and go first."

"Can't do it," Nat said smugly. "I'm the best, better even than you, Brother."

If that taunt did not snap Joseph to his senses, nothing would. I had mistaken the depths of Joseph's torment, however. Rather than proving Nat was no match for him, as we had hoped he would, Joseph cleared the board with a sweep of his arm. Chessmen went flying.

"Leave me be," he said with a snarl.

"Don't yell at Lizzie," Nat snarled back. "She's trying to help you, but all you do is treat her like dirt."

Joseph's eyes blazed. "Did I ask for your help?"

My two gentle brothers had turned into wild animals, ready to tear one another apart. This was not in the plan. I snatched up the chess pieces and put them back in place. "No, but you have it. We lost a brother, too, Joseph. We hurt the same as you."

Joseph lurched to his feet. "Not the same, Lizzie!"

I rose with him. "Don't shut us out of your life, Joseph. We love you."

"You wouldn't say that if you knew. Willie ought to be here, not me."

He felt guilty because he had survived and Willie had not, a normal reaction and a kettle of nonsense. "You both ought to be here, Joseph," I said. "The Yankees ought to be up north. This war should never have been fought. But it has, and is, and we have to accept it and hope for an end soon."

His lip curled in a sneer. "Am I to accept the fact that because of me my brother no longer lives? That I'm a cripple, hiding in a cave with women and children, like a coward?"

"No one believes you a coward," Nat said.

Joseph's voice grew quieter. "I do. I'm so ashamed."

"You've done nothing to be ashamed of," I said, managing to speak even with the fist-sized lump in my throat.

Joseph raked a hand through his hair. "The fault was mine, Lizzie. I should have saved Willie. I should have...."

My hand grazed his, to reassure, to calm. "Tell us about it, Joseph."

He hesitated only a minute. Then, slowly, with broken words and hurting heart, he shared his burden with us: "Yankees... everywhere. Guns... firing. Cannon. Minie balls whistling... so close you could feel the heat of them. The noise was deafening. Men yelling. Screaming. Bodies... everywhere. The smell of death. Fear. That was the worst part. I shall never forget the fear. You cannot imagine."

I could.

He raised his face to the sky.

I feared he would retreat into that other world and never come out. "Is that when you were wounded?" I asked to keep him with us.

Although the day was hot, his words were a whisper of ice-cold air. "It happened so fast. White-hot pain sheared through my leg. I cried out. Willie came to my aid. A second shot, meant for me, hit him. Had I not called...."

Joseph looked down at the ground. "Willie took his last breath in my arms. I tried to keep him alive until help arrived. 'Hang on, Willie. Hang on. Help us, someone. Help us.' No one came."

Joseph's shoulders shook with sobs. His tortured look begged for understanding, for forgiveness. What was there to forgive? I slid my arms around him. "You weren't at fault, Joseph." No more than I was to blame for Private Arnold, for Mack. "Had Willie been injured, you'd have done the same for him," I added.

"Small consolation. It doesn't erase the memories. They're in my head. I can't get rid of them."

"Save the pleasant memories, Joseph. They are many. Disregard the others."

"How?"

How indeed? One possibility came to mind. Joseph had always been better at drawing his thoughts than at voicing them. I went inside the cave and came back with Willie's last letter, the back of which was blank, and a pen. "Show us, Joseph. The thoughts that disturb you."

And he drew. His nightmares… his anger… his heartache. It was more terrifying than I had imagined. Soldiers on the ground, limbs twisted in grotesque shapes. Horses, their nostrils flaring. Smoke blazing from cannon and rifles. In the midst of it all, one soldier stood out, cradling another in his arms.

I heard Nat suck in air.

"Let me," he said, and I left him with his brother.

Chapter 20

WHATEVER MY BROTHERS DISCUSSED last evening—I did not ask, for Nat would share with me if he wanted—Joseph's spirits were improved the next morning. True, he wasn't laughing or talking much, but he had trimmed his whiskers and put on a fresh shirt, something he hadn't bothered with in days. And he walked partway with Papa when he left for the hospital, before the rain started. At times, he still lapsed into a disturbing silence, but he kissed me good morning. Now he and Nat sat huddled together on Joseph's mattress, in quiet conversation. I strained my ears to hear, but the steady patter, patter of raindrops on the earth above us muffled their voices.

Mama tossed my hair in a loose net. "You're awfully quiet, Elizabeth honey," she said.

I looked at her reflection in the mirror. "I was just thinking."

"What about?"

Before I could answer, the lantern she had lit to drive away the gloomy morning flickered. Something wet landed on my nose. I glanced up at the exact instant the earth gave way, and an avalanche of water burst through the ceiling.

"Mama!" Mud filled my mouth.

"Elizabeth!" She threw her arm around my neck and pulled me from under the waterfall, choking me in the process and earning herself a face full of slime and muck, and into another stream from a second crack in the ceiling.

Joseph, amazingly quick despite his leg, swept us up, one under each arm, and carried us outside. "Are you injured, Mother?"

Mama sneezed. "No, I'm all right."

Apparently satisfied she had suffered no harm Joseph pulled his shirttail out of his pants and proceeded to scrape the mud off my face with one corner. "And you, Lizzie?"

I sputtered out a mouthful of gritty water. "Let me put it this way. I'm quite delighted to have my face covered by a mask of mud, brother. Think how bewildered the nasty mosquitoes will be when they try to find soft skin to dine on."

Joseph actually laughed. Bubbles of rain flowed down his eyelashes, nose, and ears. "That's my Lizzie Tizzie. Sassy as always."

Hearing his clear laughter and seeing his crooked grin was worth a mud bath any day.

Aunt Lois found my appearance unsatisfactory, however. "You is a sight, Miss Elizabeth," she said. With her apron she scrubbed all the places on me she found unacceptable. Her thin, bony hands were firm, but loving, her words reproving yet gentle.

"Hold still, child. From the time you was a wee girl, 'fore you could even walk, you love to play in mud. I never seed such a messy child. 'Twas fate you was born a girl, 'stead of a boy."

The more she talked, the harder she scrubbed. My skin was turning pink. If she kept this up much longer, I'd be nothing but bare bones. "Ow!" I cried. "I'm clean enough, Aunt Lois. Stop. Please."

"Hush you complaining, child."

Finally, she held me at arm's length and gave me a thorough inspection. "You is presentable now, Miss Elizabeth, 'cepting for the mud in your hair."

That was good to hear. "You can help me wash it later," I said.

In the meantime, Mama was looking around, a worry line between her eyes. "Joseph, Elizabeth, have you seen Nathan?"

"Not since…." Joseph spun toward the cave.

The same scene must have whirled through our brains. Nat was buried in that mountain of mud. I lunged for the cave crying, "Nat!" and got tangled up with Mama and Joseph in their mad dash.

A faint "I'm here" floated out of the darkness.

"Go back, Lizzie, Mother," Joseph said. "The support beams aren't holding. The whole roof is about to give way. I don't want to have to dig out the three of you."

Mama and I stood nearby, our arms around each other. Uncle Morris and Aunt Lois muttered prayers.

Joseph edged forward cautiously. "Nathan," he called, "where are you?"

A mud-caked face separated itself from the soggy floor. White teeth sparkled. Brown eyes twinkled. "Wow! That was some landslide!"

Less than a minute after Joseph pulled Nat out, another section of roof crumbled. Our cave home was built to protect us. Instead, it had almost caused us serious injuries. In this upside-down world we lived in, we could trust nothing. A sad, sad thought.

Mama's mouth twitched down. Poor Nat. Now that he had been rescued and was unhurt, Mama would no doubt give him a thorough scolding for frightening the life out of her. "What in heaven's name were you thinking of, Nathan Stamford?" Mama said.

Nat, the little boy who used to hang his head at Mama's reprimands, now picked up a large object, covered with mud, and handed it to her. "I thought you'd want this," he said.

Mama scraped a clump of mud off the object. She gasped. "Nathan! It's my portrait of you children." She scuffed off more mud. Her eyes were bright with unshed tears. "You risked having the life crushed out of you to save a painting?"

Nat shoved his grimy hands in his pockets. "It's our family, Mother."

He didn't say the painting could never be replaced, but it couldn't, at any price. Willie was in it.

"I'll help you restore it, Mama," I said.

"We'll do that, honey." She held the painting as though she'd never let it out of her sight. She allowed herself a second quick look and then got back to business. Mama was doing a magnificent job of running the household in Papa's many absences.

"Morris, Dr. Stamford will be extremely anxious when he learns of the cave-in. Fetch him a message that we had an unfortunate accident, but we're fine. Joseph, go with Morris and reassure your father we don't need his assistance, or else he'll dash home when there's nothing he can do."

"Where shall we meet you?" Joseph asked.

I almost danced in circles when Mama, with only a slight pause, said, "At the house." I managed to restrain the outward me, but the inward me was happy, happy, happy.

Joseph gave me a wink, and then he hurried off with Uncle Morris.

By now, the rain had slowed to a gentle drizzle, and the Yankee batteries resumed their assault. Mama paid them no mind, another great change from the earlier days of our siege, when she vowed to live in the cave forever if necessary.

"Come along, Nathan, Elizabeth," she said. "We'll change from these wet clothes and then see about putting the house in order."

She and Aunt Lois were two or three steps ahead, when Nat seized my arm and turned me to face him. Saying nothing, he fastened Willie's star pin on my dress. I arched an eyebrow. "How did you find this in that river of mud?"

Nat lifted his shoulders in a helpless shrug. "I saw it fall off your dress when Joseph snatched you up, and something told me it was near the portrait."

I searched for the right words to express my gratitude. The usual "Thank you" seemed inadequate. For want of a better idea, I leaned forward and kissed Nat's grubby face.

He scrunched up his forehead and puckered his lips. "'Thank you' would have pleased me, Lizzie."

೮つび

The house had suffered additional damage since our last visit. The front windowpanes were all broken. I could only guess about the ones in back. At least four new holes marked the passage of shells through the walls. Visions of my piano in shambles sent me racing to the parlor. Only a layer of plaster on top marred its beautiful wood. The second floor, where puddles of water stood from the rain that leaked through holes in the roof, was the worst.

We spent the morning cleaning, after which I climbed the oak tree to see the baby birds. Feathers, instead of fuzz, covered their tiny bodies, but they opened their beaks the same as before. A few more days and they'd fly away. I stroked a silky head and wished that I could travel to some quiet and peaceful place with them.

Suddenly, angry voices swelled below me, making the birds shrink into their nest and me to glance down.

"Absolutely not!" Joseph shouted.

"If you can, I can," Nat shouted back.

"They won't allow it. You're only twelve."

"Thirteen next month."

I knew at once what they were arguing about. So Nat fancied joining the army, did he? After all he had heard and seen? I'd never comprehend his thinking. As for Joseph, wasn't his crippled leg enough? Did he wish to lose his limbs completely? Ignoring the fact that I once had wanted to be a soldier, I tossed a twig at them, hitting Nat on top of the head. He glanced up, scowling.

"You're both out of your minds," I said. "You, Nat, are too young to entertain such absurd notions. And you, Joseph, have a bad leg that is far from well. You can hardly walk. How do you expect to keep up with your regiment?"

"You, Lizzie, are a meddlesome sister," Joseph said. "Now get out of that tree. My neck is cramping looking up at you."

"Meddlesome, am I?" I dropped down. "If you haven't the sense of a chicken, who hasn't the sense to come in out of the rain, then someone has to meddle in your affairs and prevent you from doing something foolish."

"Mind your own business, Lizzie," Joseph said, his jaw dancing.

He had forgotten I shared the same obstinate heritage as he. My own jaw did a lively bit of polka. "Insufferable, pigheaded, and you hush your mouth, Nat," I said, never giving him a chance to say whatever he might consider saying.

I propped my hands on my hips. "Since you're about making yourselves heroes, I shan't try to stop you. In fact, I'm going with you. Nat, I wish to borrow your trousers again."

"You didn't borrow them before," Nat said. "You stole them."

Anticipating his answer, I was already on my way to the house.

"Why do you want Nathan's trousers?" Joseph asked, at my heel as I trotted up the porch steps.

"To be a man," I said. "I told you in my letters."

Joseph pursued me into Nat's room. "I never received your letters."

I pulled a pair of pants out of Nat's armoire.

"No one will believe you're a man, Lizzie," Joseph said. "You are decidedly a girl, with long hair and… and other things."

Nat grabbed the trousers from my hands. "We won't let you," he said.

"You won't let me? Oh! I see. It's permissible for you two to go gallivanting around the countryside, Yankees taking potshots at you, but not for me, since I'm a girl."

"Girls are too fragile for war," Joseph said. "Girls are meant to cook and wash and sew and…."

"I can't believe my own brother spouting such nonsense," I said. "For your information, Joseph Stamford, women have enlisted in the army. Those women shoot as straight, march as far, and fight as bravely as any man. They have to hide their identity because of attitudes like yours. I'm a Stamford, too, in case you've forgotten. I shall do as I please."

I turned my back on my brothers to let my temper cool. My hands trembled when I undressed.

"If I have to lock you in the water closet to keep you here, I will," Joseph said, threatening.

I latched onto Nat's trousers and pulled them on, along with one of his shirts. "I shall climb out the window."

"You'll break your neck," Nat said.

"It's my neck." I piled my hair on my head, pinned it. I held out my hand. "Your cap please."

Not waiting for his tart "No," I grabbed Nat's cap and covered my hair. But I had not counted on the images that rolled through my mind when I was dressed like a man again: Private Arnold, eyes blank, Ben's arm, green, pulpy and bloody. I sank down on Nat's bed.

"What is it, Lizzie," Joseph said. "You look like you've seen a ghost."

"I have," I whispered.

"Nathan, get her a glass of water."

"No water." I folded my hands. "Let me tell you about Private Arnold, and Mack, and Ben."

And I did.

By the time I finished, Joseph was shaking his head in disbelief. "I had no idea," he said. He twisted a loose wisp of my hair around his finger. "My brave little sister. When I was at the hospital with Father, I saw the wounded men, Lizzie. Some will never rise from their bed, but I can walk. I can fire a gun. I must go for them and for Willie and you."

"Then let's be on our way."

"You're serious?"

"Absolutely."

"So am I," Nat said.

Joseph crinkled his nose. Said nothing for a moment. Then softly said, "We do have a cave to repair."

"The cave is more dangerous than the house," I said. "You can fix it all you want, but from now on, I plan to sleep in my own bed."

He gave me a half-smile. "Then pray the skies stay clear, Lizzie Tizzie. Your room has a hole directly above your bed."

"I'll move the bed, or patch the hole, or cover it with my parasol."

"All in good time," Joseph said. "But the cave comes first."

Nat dragged a hand over his brow. "I'm glad you settled that, brother. I never fancied being a soldier."

Joseph's smile disappeared. "Few men, North or South, want to fight, Nathan. They'd prefer to stay home with their families. But sometimes circumstances rage out of our control, and we're trapped in the madness. Sometimes it changes a man, not always for the better. Then we find out what we're really made of."

"Women, too," I said, thinking of Mama. But Joseph had me in mind.

He raised my hand and kissed it. "You're made of loyalty and courage, Lizzie. You never gave up on me."

"I said some unkind words about you."

"All of them true, I'm sure."

"At the time they were."

Light footfalls sounded in the hallway, and, with a rustle of crinolines, Mama swished into the room. "Here you are, Elizabeth. Honey, a young soldier has come to call on you. He...."

She made a funny grunt and clutched her throat. Her gaze traveled over me. "Oh, dear! What have you done to yourself, Elizabeth? Those are... men's clothes."

Her words passed over my head, for I was in a daze at her announcement. The soldier had to be Ben. He was here, to see me. Not questioning the wisdom of his visit or why he was here, I cried, "Ben," and flew around Mama, but got no farther than the top of the stairs, where Joseph caught up with me.

"A young lady does not greet a gentleman caller wearing men's clothes and without a chaperone." Joseph turned me around, marched me into Nat's room, and picked my dress up from the floor. "We shall wait for you at the stairs."

Anxious to see Ben and grumbling at the delay, I wiggled into my dress, leaving off the crinolines, took a moment to straighten my hair, and then rushed to the staircase. My three chaperones accompanied me to the parlor. I'd hear from Mama about my appearance later, after Ben was gone. But I didn't care.

Ben, however, was not the soldier in the parlor.

Chapter 21

A CONFEDERATE SOLDIER, standing by the fireplace, removed his cap, held it in front of him, and bowed. "Mrs. Stamford, Miss Stamford. Excuse me for intruding, but I have a letter, most urgent, I believe, for you, Miss." He strode directly to me and offered me an envelope.

My mouth fell open, and I stared in surprise at the piece of paper. Was the soldier daft? My only correspondence had been with my brothers. Who else would write to me? I couldn't think of a single soul. Save for... Miriam's round little face and turned-up nose flitted through my mind. How silly of me. The letter was from her, of course. But who was this fellow delivering it? He was one of her beaus probably, attracted like dozens of others by her molasses-colored hair, dimpled cheeks, and fluttery lashes. All her life, young men had flocked around Miriam, treating her like a princess, doing her every bidding. I must learn her secret. Eyeing her latest conquest with curiosity and admiration, I reached out and relieved him of the envelope.

"Is Miriam well, Lieutenant?" I noted the two bars on each of his collars. "When does her family plan to return to Vicksburg? She is my dear friend, you know. Where did you two meet?"

"Elizabeth!" Mama broke in. "Give the poor lieutenant a chance to catch his breath."

I forced my mouth to take a rest.

Now that I had stopped running on, Mama introduced us. "Children, this is Lieutenant Leroy Quinn, from Louisiana. I'm sure he'll tell us all about himself, Elizabeth, if you have patience, and mind your conduct." She whispered that last part in my ear.

She turned her most charming smile on our guest. "You must be hot and tired, Lieutenant. We'll take tea. Sit down, everyone. Nathan, tell Lois to prepare an extra cup. I hope sassafras is satisfactory, Lieutenant."

"Sassafras is fine, Ma'am."

Joseph and Lieutenant Quinn remained standing until Mama and I were seated, and then they sat, the lieutenant in a chair opposite us, Joseph on the arm of the sofa. I pinched my lips together to stifle the words attempting to spring forth and tapped my foot impatiently, as Mama asked Lieutenant Quinn about his family and numerous other unimportant things. My fingers itched to tear into the letter. I had heard nothing from Miriam since her family left Vicksburg, and I missed the hours we spent together, sewing, gossiping, and reading *Godey's Lady's Book* to see the new fashions and stories. I could remain silent only so long.

During a lull in the conversation, I sneaked in a word or two. "Lieutenant Quinn, are you sweet on Miriam?"

A sudden coughing spell wracked the lieutenant's body. He formed a circle with his fist, pressed it against his lips, until the coughs died down. His eyes, a lovely smoky gray, sparkled with what I could only identify as amusement.

The lieutenant cleared his throat. "Pardon me, Miss Stamford. I must have swallowed something. I'm not acquainted with this Miriam you mention, so I certainly am not sweet on her, or on any girl for that matter. A Yankee, who claimed he was a friend of yours, bade me fetch you the dispatch."

Mama seized my arm to silence me from further embarrassing our guest, or myself, I suppose.

"You say my daughter's letter is from a Yankee?" she asked.

"Yes, Ma'am."

A Yankee, not Miriam, had written my message. I was more puzzled than ever. Unless…. Good gracious me! Was it Ben? I darted another look at the envelope, at the small, precise print that spelled my name. Ben's signature was in the upper corner, neat and polite, so like him. A part of me itched to tear it open immediately, to read his words, but another part of me said to wait. Letters weren't always good news. Sometimes they brought pain and sorrow. I decided to read it later in the solitude of my room, after our guest departed.

Manners obliged me to thank the lieutenant, but one glance at the thin laugh lines crinkled at the edges of his eyes and I changed my mind. "Do you find me amusing, lieutenant?"

To credit him with some manners of his own, he answered me politely and honestly, his voice soft as silk cloth, a true Southern gentleman. "Forgive me if I've embarrassed you, Miss Elizabeth. You do not mind that I call you Elizabeth?" he asked, and went right on without waiting for my approval. "I assure you I do not find you amusing, just"—he searched for a word—"astonishing."

"Astonishing?" I couldn't conclude whether that was good or bad.

He winced, blew out a puff of air, and clapped his hand on his leg. "I did it again. My incompetence around a fair lady rules my tongue. May we start over, pretend we just met, which in fact we have?"

In spite of my irritation with him, I hid a smile behind my hand. If I kept having need of a fan, I must learn to carry one. I glanced at Mama. She nodded. "If you wish," I said.

He rose, came over, stood before me, and bowed slightly. He spoke to me as though we were the only two people in the room. "Lieutenant Leroy Quinn delighted to make your acquaintance, Miss Elizabeth. I meant to say you are a most handsome, amiable, fascinating girl, exactly what I expected after seeing the daguerreotype of you and hearing about you from the Yankee."

"You know Ben?" I asked.

"In a manner of speaking, yes," the lieutenant said.

"This is the wounded young man you brought home for your father to attend, is he not, Elizabeth?" Mama asked.

"He is. Benjamin Clayton."

Joseph's narrowed eyes and sour expression were an obvious indication he didn't credit everything the lieutenant was saying. He wasted words no more than did Nat, especially when he was being the protective older brother.

"It strikes me as rather odd that you should have a photograph of my sister, Lieutenant, since you obviously have never met her,"

Joseph said bluntly. "And another thing doesn't ring true. I find it strange that a Yankee bade you, a Confederate officer, to fetch my sister a letter, and even stranger that you agreed."

Lieutenant Quinn answered without blinking an eye, which in my opinion meant he was being truthful. I should recognize the difference between a lie and the truth, since I was familiar with both.

"The daguerreotype doesn't belong to me but to the Yankee," Lieutenant Quinn said. "It's now in his possession. As for the letter, considering what Private Clayton did for me I couldn't with clear conscience refuse to honor his request."

"What did Ben do?" I asked, fascinated by this young officer.

"I am alive today because of that Yankee."

Joseph's brows knit together. "I can accept the fact that the Yankee, Private Clayton, saved your life, but that doesn't explain where he came by Lizzie's picture."

"He did not say."

They all focused their attention on me, as though words of wisdom would spill from my mouth to reveal the secrets of the universe. Imagine their disappointment when I only shrugged and said, "The last I saw of my photograph it was on the washstand in my room." To move them away from me to a more important topic, I asked the lieutenant, "How did Ben save you?"

"It's a long, complicated story, Miss Elizabeth."

"We have nothing but time," Mama said, a hint of curiosity in her voice.

"Do tell us." I was eager to know everything, but rather than letting Lieutenant Quinn talk, I found myself rattling on, as usual. "Has Ben heard from his mother and father? Is his arm whole? He didn't lose it, I hope. He was so worried the surgeons would cut it off."

Patiently the lieutenant put my every concern to rest. "Private Clayton had two arms and two of everything else he was supposed to have when I saw him. However, for the rest of your questions, may I suggest the letter will better inform you than I."

Nat swung into the parlor, carrying a tray of mismatched cups and a pot of tea, right on time to stick his nose where it had no business. He plunked the tray on the table. "Does the Yank matter to you, Lizzie?"

He must have been listening in the hallway. He would forever blame Ben for what happened in Virginia. In the beginning I felt the same. I couldn't deny that for the rest of my life I'd resent the fact my darling Willie's life had been snuffed out so cruelly, but I was learning to accept what I couldn't change. The passage of time had dulled the pain, made it somewhat bearable. Placing fault would not bring him back. If anything, it kept the heartache fresh. Willie still lived in my heart—nobody could take him from me—and I would not tarnish his memory with bitter feelings. I shut my ears to Nat's hostile words.

When I got up to help Mama pour tea, the lieutenant and Joseph bounded up. I waved them to their seats. Despite my good intentions, I was unable to control my blistering tongue, and I lit into my brother. "I care about Ben! So do you, Nat, save you're too stubborn to admit it. Or do you not remember your plans to travel to the stars with him?"

I was so furious I accidentally splashed hot tea on the lieutenant's hand. "Forgive me!" I cried. I wiped my skirt at the red streak spreading across his palm. "It looks awful! May I put salve or something on it to stop the burn?"

Lieutenant Quinn's eyes watered like a leaky bucket, but he laughed it off. "Don't fret, Miss Elizabeth. I've had worse injuries."

Nat wasn't laughing. "The moon, Lizzie," he said, correcting me. "We were flying to the moon; but that was before. I also remember Willie. Do you?"

His words stung and I lashed out to hurt him the way he was hurting me. "How dare you say such a horrid thing! I ought to rip out your hateful tongue for being so cruel!"

Mama stepped in to break up our quarrel. She gathered up the cups, placed them on the tray, and shoved it at Nat. "I cannot abide cold tea, Nathan," she said. "Run to the kitchen and tell Lois we'd like hot."

Nat glared at me, but followed Mama's orders. She was a clever lady. Nat never stayed angry for long; neither did I. A few minutes apart would cool us both down, and then we'd apologize and all would be forgiven. Mama was a born peacemaker. Presidents Abraham Lincoln and Jefferson Davis should take a lesson from her. Then this war would be a short one.

I gulped in several quick breaths to let my temper return to normal. I then retired to the sofa with Mama and Joseph.

"Forgive us for the interruption, Lieutenant," Mama said. "You were about to tell us of your experience with Private Clayton. We're very interested."

Lieutenant Quinn glanced at each of us, including Nat who had silently slipped into the parlor and stood just within the door. Nat mouthed an apology to me, which I acknowledged by beckoning him to sit beside me. When he was settled, the lieutenant began his journey into the past and what brought him and Ben's letter to our house.

Although Lieutenant Quinn spoke to all of us, he directed his gaze at me. "What I am about to say may seem incredible. I find it hard to believe myself, but I owe my life to a Yankee, and I shan't ever forget him or what he did for me."

I leaned forward.

His eyes locked onto mine, drawing me to the very place where he and Ben had met. I could almost smell the musty leaves and charred meat, and feel the hot, sultry air. My spine tingled as his soft southern voice spun his story. "Two days ago I was scouting a new location, in search of a better vantage point to observe the movement of Federal gunboats, when I caught the scent of something burning. I gave it little thought at first. Smoke from cannon fire and mortar shells is common in the air, and I should not have noticed, save that a hint of something enticingly like meat tickled my nostrils. Curious, I decided to investigate, which turned out to be a bad mistake on my part, for I stumbled onto a campfire, where four Yankees were roasting a small rabbit at the end of a stick. Before I was able to retreat, the nearest soldier spied me."

"Ben," we all said.

"Private Clayton wasn't with the Yankees at this point."

"They took you prisoner then," Joseph said.

Lieutenant Quinn focused on Joseph. "From the quick way they drew their rifles on me, I suspect their intentions were more deadly. I don't know what they were doing away from their company, perhaps on a foraging expedition or some other mission, but they didn't seem inclined to take any prisoners. The soldier who had spied me leveled his gun at me. The other men charged to their feet, hammers on weapons clinking, all aimed in my direction. I scarcely moved a muscle. With one soldier I had a chance. Four would cut me down before I fired a shot. You can bet I was quite worried, so I said a prayer."

I had to shake myself out of that scene, out of the whine of bullets whizzing past my ears, hitting their targets, shattering bones and lives. My throat was tight, and I studied the lieutenant's earnest face. He was reliving the moment, the way the past sometimes still tortured Joseph. "How dreadful for you, lieutenant," I said. "How did you get away?"

"Private Clayton answered my prayer."

Nat snorted. "He's a Yankee. Why would he help you?"

I gripped Nat's hand. He grew quiet.

"Like you, Nathan, I believed he was just another Yankee eager to put a bullet in me." Lieutenant Quinn rubbed his chin, his neck. "Clayton walked into camp, attracted as I was by the tempting aroma of food," he said, "though I hear the Yankees have no shortage of supplies, at least compared to our army. He said nothing to me, but I noted the side-glances he kept sending my way, as if he was trying to communicate. Whatever he had in mind couldn't be good for me, I figured, so I kept a wary eye on him. My legs were falling asleep from standing so still. If the Yanks proposed to shoot me, then get on with it. At the present, however, the rabbit interested them more than a Reb. They tied me to a tree and proceeded to eat."

By now I was perched on the edge of the sofa, hanging on his every word. And I knew. "Ben helped you escape."

Lieutenant Quinn favored me with a smile. "I do believe the Yankee is part Southern. He convinced the other soldiers that a boat transporting the foe to prison was departing immediately, and he would see me on it. They could go on about their business, without the worry of a prisoner, or a body to dispose of. Paying no attention to their warnings about watching the … um … Reb in words I shan't repeat before ladies, Clayton removed me from the tree, tied my hands behind my back, and we walked some distance down the road. I was suspicious as to what his game was. Did he want the glory of killing me himself, displaying my sword as his trophy? I was more than nervous, I admit, but facing one Yankee was better than five, so I went meekly, planning to overpower him at the first opportunity. When he ordered me to stop, I decided to make my move, lest my only chance of escape passed me by."

Mama's fan had been beating wildly. It now stood still. "Private Clayton untied you," she said.

"He handed me my musket," the lieutenant said.

"And set you free." I gave Nat a meaningful look.

"Not right away. Clayton pulled your photograph from his pocket, Miss Elizabeth, and asked if I was acquainted with you. I suppose he thought I was from Vicksburg. I informed him I had not had the pleasure, though I'd very much like to. We talked pleasantly for a while, during the course of which he told me about your loss. I am truly sad for you." He cast a look at Mama. "For all of you."

The memory of how gently Ben had held me when we learned about Willie stirred a tenderness inside me. "He set you free, lieutenant, for Willie, and for me."

Mama rested a comforting hand on mine. Nat and Joseph were terribly quiet. Thinking, I suppose.

"Clayton is troubled in regard to your safety, Miss Elizabeth," Lieutenant Quinn said. "The reason for his dispatch, I believe."

"If he's concerned about my welfare, why did he not fetch me the letter himself?"

"He was afraid you'd not receive him."

Ben could not know how wrong he was.

Chapter 22

THE MINUTE LIEUTENANT QUINN departed I raced to my room, flung myself across the bed, and commenced to read:

June 1863

Dear Elizabeth,

I hope by now you've forgiven me for being a Yankee. What I told you earlier is still true. I stand ready to provide whatever aid you need.

Again, I offer my condolences in the loss of your brother. I think I should have liked him, and he, me, had we been granted the privilege of knowing each other.

Do you believe in destiny? I do. For instance, I was sent to Vicksburg, wounded, and nursed by you, as though a guiding hand led us to one another. I hear your laughter of disbelief, but 'tis true. You told me yourself that your father is a Yankee.

It seems we Yankees are decidedly struck with Southern girls.

I have some news that may upset you, but you ought to be aware of. Our men have begun tunneling to get closer to Confederate lines. When the ditches are complete, we will blow up the Confederate works. Vicksburg cannot survive much longer.

I regret my part in adding more sorrow to your already burdened heart, but I took the oath to honor my country. So I shall.

I hear disturbing reports you have little food, and some citizens are eating rats. Don't, Elizabeth. I'll share

my rations with you, as soon as I'm able to obtain leave.
I do plan to call on you, for I have something to return
to you. I have no regrets for borrowing your picture. It
has given me hope and courage during those long, dark
nights in the rifle pits.

One day, when you're older, would you consider visiting my home in Ohio? My mother and father would
delight in making your acquaintance. Think about it.
Will you? Until I see you again.

Your friend,
Ben

"May I enter?" Nat asked.

I was aware he had been watching me from the hallway for quite
some time. I pushed up on my bed, where I was lying. "You don't
have to ask, Nat."

He shuffled in, his hands in his pockets. He scuffed his foot back
and forth, his head down. "Will you go to Ohio with the Yankee?"
he asked, as if the world would suddenly end if I did.

Poor forlorn little boy. I could not yet think of him as a man.
He looked so sad. I reached out and lifted his chin. "You're wearing
your gloomy face again," I said. "I have no plans to leave Vicksburg,
with Ben or anybody else. I have to watch out for you and Joseph
and keep you out of trouble."

Nat's mouth curved in his sweet smile. "You're a bit mixed-up,
aren't you, Lizzie? You're the one who's always in trouble."

"My point exactly. We need each other; so don't go inviting worries where there are none. Nat, is it true? Are people eating rats?"

"Where did you hear that?"

"Ben. He asked me not to."

"Uncle Morris says they are. Some claim rat meat tastes like
squirrel." Nat wrinkled his nose. "I'd rather starve. I can't stand mule
meat, either."

"Where's Joseph?" I asked mainly to get our minds off the subject of rats as a meal. "I haven't seen him since Lieutenant Quinn took his leave."

"Joseph went off with his rifle."

"To where?"

"He didn't say, but he was mumbling you were too thin and should eat more."

That night we dined on a wild turkey that, despite the hungry soldiers and flying bullets, managed to stay alive until Joseph went hunting. Against my brother's expert marksmanship the bird stood no chance. It was the most delicious meal I had ever eaten. Even the cornbread we had with it tasted magnificent.

For the first time in weeks I went to bed with my stomach full, burrowed under the soft white sheets and feather pillows and smiled dreamily at the white canopy above me, safe now under the ceiling my brothers repaired. The night air was warm, but I breathed easily, without choking on dust. I was content, yet I couldn't help but wonder what would happen when the war was over. If the North won, would some Yankee move into our house? Sleep in my bed? If so, where would we go? But that wasn't about to happen. Ben was wrong; the South would win. Those pleasant thoughts and the gentle breeze soon sang me to sleep.

My bed lurched, waking me with a start. Cannon roared and I dashed, screaming, to Mama's room and leapt into bed with her.

"Oh! Oh! Oh!" she squealed right along with me, until her wits came back and she realized it was me. She snuggled me close. "Elizabeth honey, you gave me a fright."

"The cannon, Mama! I hate them!"

Another blast shook the walls and rattled my teeth. A flash of light danced across the room, and seconds later Nat and Joseph bolted in, their bodies tangling in the doorway as they pushed through at the same instant.

"Mother!" Joseph said, looking somewhat sheepish. "I thought you might be scared."

She sat up. "Joseph, Nathan, there's plenty of room."

The bed groaned under their weight when they crowded in, Joseph on Mama's right, Nat wriggling under her arm that had been around me. "Move over, Lizzie," he said.

I wasn't about letting him get away with that. I gave him a shove that landed him with a thump on the floor. "Find your own arm, thief. I was here first."

Nat crawled onto Mama's lap, his lip puckered. "Actually Joseph is the oldest," he said, "which makes him here first."

I had to get in the last word. "In any case, you're the last."

Mama smiled wistfully. "I used to wish I had four arms, one for each of my children." She sighed, kissed each of us. "May God watch over William in his lonesome grave."

Joseph wrapped all three of us in his long arms. With gentle assurances he said, "Willie isn't alone, Mother. He has us, and he's here now, in our midst. I can feel him. Lie still and you will, too."

An eerie quietness hovered in the air, as if the room were listening. Even the war without the walls grew silent. A sense of peace surrounded me, like the music of a tender lullaby. Perhaps Willie was with us, in spirit, the way he had promised, but it wasn't the same.

Chapter 23

AGAINST MY VIGOROUS PROTESTS, which fell on deaf ears, when morning light dawned, Joseph, Nat, Uncle Morris, and I waded through pools of muddy rainwater to see what repairs the cave required. As we approached that mountain of soggy earth, I cried out with delight, "What a mess! We can't live here save we're fish or alligators. Since we are neither...."

I turned to retreat, but Joseph had to go and say, "We Stamfords never say can't, Lizzie."

He did know how to get to me. I had a thing or two to say, myself. I spun back, folded my arms. "Is that so? You fancy telling me then how you plan to clean up this disgusting, disagreeable place? Dig it out one handful at a time?"

Joseph raked a hand through his hair, making it stand on end. "Now there's a thought."

He was jesting, at least I hoped he was and I hadn't put ideas into his head. I ought to learn to control my tongue, but that called for a miracle. We had had few of those lately. Joseph ascended to the grassy top of the cave and walked back and forth, pausing in spots and tapping the ground with the heel of his boot. He came down, went partway inside the cave, and ran his fingers over what appeared to be cracks in the wall, though he wouldn't allow Nat or me close enough to get a good look.

After he completed his survey, he announced the walls and ceiling were in no danger of giving way further. It was safe for us to proceed. He grinned at me. "I do have a better idea than using our hands, Lizzie."

He tossed me one of two spades Uncle Morris had been carrying. "You and I will scoop out the mud, and then we'll patch the walls. Nathan, you help Uncle Morris repair the roof."

Scoop mud? Patch cracks? Had I considered it carefully, I should have known what the spades were for. Joseph was crazy. I flung the spade to the ground, kicked it aside, and shook my head. "I'll get my dress dirty," I said in protest. "And what if the rest of the earth collapses? Would it make you happy to see my brains splattered against the walls?"

"When did you ever fret about your appearance, Lizzie?" Joseph asked. I must have looked so distressed that he added, much more kindly, "You think I'd risk your life? I'll be right beside you."

"Lizzie's right," Nat said, adding his cent's worth. "Digging in mud is too hard a task for a lady. Let her work with Uncle Morris."

I stomped my foot. "Too hard for ladies, is it? I'll have you know I'm not some fragile creature who cannot even turn a clump of earth. I've done it plenty of times in my garden."

A sly grin passed between my brothers, and I snatched up the spade and commenced to prove my point. Or was I proving theirs?

"That's the spirit, Lizzie Tizzie," Joseph said, shoveling alongside me. "I shan't allow anything bad to happen to you. Life would be boring without you around."

More teasing, a glorious recovery for Joseph. The phantoms were still there, of course, always would be, I suppose, but he was facing them and dealing with them. I huffed and puffed. Perspiration beaded on my brow. I loved being able to jest with him. The least I could do was to give him a taste of his own medicine. "I'll try to live up to your expectations. That is a promise, Brother Dear."

He chuckled. "Thanks for the warning."

I shoveled mud and dirt and considered the many changes this war had brought to not only Joseph but to my whole family. Nat had grown into a young man, and Willie.... Whenever I thought about him, emptiness crept through me. Would it ever go away? Impulsively, I threw my arms around Joseph and buried my face against his chest.

For a moment he didn't move, then he kissed the top of my head, stroked my hair, and whispered, "I know, Lizzie," and we went back to work.

Above us, Uncle Morris sang in his deep, pleasant voice, pausing at times to give Nat instructions, reminding me of my earlier conversation with Ben. I, the terribly spoiled only daughter, had changed perhaps the most. I was more conscious of other people's feelings now and saw Aunt Lois and Uncle Morris in a different light. They were more than servants to do my bidding. They were people, like me. Were they truly happy with us? They never complained, but perhaps Ben was right, and they would prefer living in their own home, planting their own gardens. I sensed this war would bring changes to their lives as well as ours. Nothing would ever be the same, for anyone.

A few days later, we took possession of the cave. Again.

Chapter 24

"DO YOU HEAR IT, Lizzie?" Nat asked.

We were sitting on the sloping hillside, close by the cave, Nat carving a new flying machine and I mending a tear in Joseph's shirt. I looked up and listened. A bird twittered in the nearby trees; otherwise, the day was as still as a graveyard. "The cannon are quiet," I said. "What does it mean?"

Nat sprang to his feet. "I'm not sure. Let's ask Mother."

But Mama hushed us the instant we entered the cave. "Don't come any closer," she whispered from her rocking chair, where she crouched, her hands clenched in tight balls in her lap.

I soon saw the reason why. I mashed my hand over my mouth. "Nat," I said between my fingers.

"I see it. Keep still, Mother."

Keep still? That was easy for him to say. He wasn't the one in the rocker, with a snake half as long as he was tall coiled beneath it. Mama was.

"Be careful, Nat," I said.

He glanced my way. "Stay cool, Lizzie. We don't wish to excite the snake."

I shook my head. We did not wish to do that.

With one eye on the reptile, Nat inched toward Joseph's sword propped against the wall. The snake's beady eyes seemed to track his movement.

Nat's intentions were good, but I had no doubt his love of animals would prevent him from harming the snake. He'd more than likely decide to make it a pet. Unlike Nat, I had no qualms about smashing the creature flat. I scanned the cave for a weapon, spied the skillet within arm's reach, and snatched it up, forgetting Nat's warning to stay cool.

The snake uncoiled.

Nat shouted, "Stand back, Lizzie!" and swooped the sword down. He missed.

The snake slithered aside, unharmed.

Mama threw her fan, hitting the snake on its back. "Get away from my children, you nasty creature!"

The snake, either confused or angry, headed straight for Nat. I jumped forward and swung the skillet with all my strength. The blow only grazed the creature's head. I raised the skillet to strike again, but Nat was faster. With one swift stroke, he brought the sword down on target. The snake's head rolled, as did my stomach.

Afterward, Nat turned green and thudded to the floor. Weeping softly, Mama knelt on one side of him. I crouched on the other. She planted a light kiss on his cheek. If anything revived him, that display of emotions would.

Sure enough, his eyes flapped open. He swiped a hand over his face. "Mother! I'm all right. Honest."

As soon as Nat convinced Mama the snake had not bitten him, she ordered him to dispose of "that slithery varmint."

Nat was on his feet by then, eyeing the snake's remains. "Sorry, but it was either my mother and sister or you. I fancy them, so you lost."

He carried the snake outside and buried it under the sassafras tree. He said a few words about how the snake shouldn't have invaded our home, and he hoped its death had been painless.

Joseph limped up soon after we had finished sprinkling earth over the creature. He frowned. "Your fingernails have enough dirt under them to grow a field of corn, Lizzie. Yours are even worse, Nathan. What mischief have you two been up to now?"

"Nat's a hero," I said.

Joseph's eyebrow shot up. "A hero is he?"

"You should have seen him. There was this gigantic snake, this big." I opened my arms wide, exaggerating the snake's size only a little, and related the events.

Joseph rumpled Nat's hair. "Well done, brother."

"Where were you? Nat asked, his ears a bright pink at Joseph's praise.

"At the hospital with Father." Joseph put a hand on each of our shoulders. "Lizzie, Nathan, I have news. Father received word that General Pemberton and General Grant are meeting this afternoon to negotiate terms of surrender."

"Who's surrendering?" Nat asked. "Them or us?"

An incredible sadness darkened Joseph's eyes. "Pemberton gave up."

Joseph rubbed his bad leg. "In fairness to the general, he had little choice. Johnston never came to our aid. Our army's rations are almost nonexistent. The men are ill and dying for want of medicine. Many are deserting, I hear. Who can fault them?" He looked out over the town and breathed in, a long, ragged breath. "Heaven help me, but I'm glad it's over."

Mama rubbed Joseph's broad back. "I wish the peace had come sooner," she said.

I put my arm around her. "What day is it?" I asked.

"The third of July."

Nat pushed out his lower lip. "We might have surrendered, but Willie would say we're not whipped. We're just smart enough to know when to stop."

❧❧

On the Fourth of July, after forty-seven days of constant bombardment, the siege of Vicksburg ended. Around ten o'clock that morning, Mama, Papa, Joseph, Nat, and I walked to the courthouse. Along the way we saw white flags waving above the Confederate works. Arms were stacked in the streets, but our brave soldiers held their heads high. Many were so overcome with emotion that tears streamed down their faces. Others were not quite as ready to admit defeat. They smashed their muskets rather than surrender them. My heart broke for them. Once, we were confident we were in the right, and we would win. Now, like Papa said ages ago, I wondered if there was a right or a wrong side, or only men's beliefs. And those were far from perfect.

When the Federal troops marched into the city, I had to accept the fact Vicksburg had fallen. We were among the few citizens who watched our Stars and Bars lowered from the flagpole. Most stayed home, preferring to observe from their galleries or to shut out the sight behind closed windows. The men in blue raised the Stars and Stripes. The Union band played "Yankee Doodle," "The Star Spangled Banner," and other songs. The Yankee soldiers seemed to feel the defeated army's sorrow and offered not a taunt or unkind word to our men, at least not so I heard.

"The war has ended," Nat said.

"For Vicksburg it has," Joseph said.

Across the way a Federal soldier disengaged from a wall of blue coats and strode toward us. My heart tripped against my ribs. "Ben."

Nat nudged me. From the ragged gray ranks, Lieutenant Leroy Quinn strolled in our direction. I touched Willie's star pin on my dress. North and South, together again. Somehow, it seemed right.

I cannot say what will happen next, but whatever comes we will survive. We have proven we can.

The End

Author Bio

Beverly Stowe McClure is a native Texan. She lives in the country, outside of Iowa Park, with her husband, Jack, and a cat named Sugar, who isn't really sweet. She has three sons, four granddaughters and two grandsons. She also has a great-grandson. (She married very young.)

She earned a BSEd from Midwestern State University. Her stories and articles have appeared in leading children's magazines.

Beverly is a member of both the North Texas and the national Society of Children's Book Writers and Illustrators. She is currently working on two historical novels for children, as well as a couple of picture books.

To relax she plays the piano and tries to make flowers grow under the hot Texas sun and with little water. And she's discovered many interesting ancestors in her genealogy research.

Don't miss any of these other
exciting Young Adult novels

➢ Dragon's Moon
(1-933353-53-8, $14.95 US)

➢ Listen to the Ghost
(1-933353-51-1, $16.95 US)

➢ Nine Lives and Three Wishes
(1-933353-55-4, $13.50 US)

➢ Rebel in Blue Jeans
(1-933353-49-X, $14.95 US)

➢ Saga of Rim
(1-933353-50-3, $16.95 US)

➢ Valley of the Raven
(1-933353-75-9, $16.95 US)

➢ You, Me, Naideen and a Bee
(1-60619-208-5, $18.95 US)

Twilight Times Books
Kingsport, Tennessee

Order Form

If not available from your local bookstore or favorite online bookstore, send this coupon and a check or money order for the retail price plus $3.50 s&h to Twilight Times Books, Dept. LS710 POB 3340 Kingsport TN 37664. Delivery may take up to two weeks.

Name: _____

Address: _____

_____

Email: _____

I have enclosed a check or money order in the amount of

$_____

for _____ .

If you enjoyed this book, please post a
review at your favorite online bookstore.

Twilight Times Books
P O Box 3340
Kingsport, TN 37664
Phone/Fax: 423-323-0183
www.twilighttimesbooks.com/

CPSIA information can be obtained
at www.ICGtesting.com
Printed in the USA
EDOW022044200213
707ED